WILD LIGHTS

TYSON WILD BOOK THIRTY FIVE

TRIPP ELLIS

TRIPP ELLIS

1

"Think of it as a vacation," Sheriff Daniels said.

"When I think of a vacation, that's not what I think of," I replied.

"It's a simple little case, and after all you two have been through recently, you could use a little *simple*."

I wasn't going to argue.

"Besides, she worked so hard on the stuff. She lost her daughter last year in a car accident, and I just feel bad for her. I told her I'd put my best deputies on it." He paused, then said with a sigh. "I guess I could give it to Erickson and Faulkner."

Daniels knew how to get to me. "No, we'll take it."

Daniels had a slight grin in his voice, proud of his persuasive ability. "I want you to catch these little bastards and nail their asses to the wall. They've caused a lot of property damage. These displays aren't cheap."

"You got it, boss," I said before ending the call.

I dialed JD and filled him in on the situation. He swung by the marina and picked me up not long after. But he wasn't in his usual ride.

The car he was currently driving was a far cry from his normal style. It lacked the outrageousness required. Jack couldn't drive a regular car. It needed to be bold, fast, loud, and exotic. And it was almost criminal to drive a car in Coconut Key without a retractable top.

I grabbed my weapon, press-checked it, holstered it in my waistband for an appendix carry, and hustled down the dock to the parking lot. It was a beautiful day—a cool 73° with only a few wispy clouds in the sky. Boats swayed in their slips, gulls squawked overhead, and waves gently lapped against fiberglass hulls in the marina.

JD pulled into the parking lot, driving a silver four-door econobox with tires just a tad wider than a bicycle's.

I had to chuckle.

It was average as average could be. Nothing about JD was ever *average*.

I didn't have much room to talk.

It was better than my car.

I didn't have a car.

I pulled open the door and climbed into the passenger seat. "How much longer are you going to drive this?"

JD frowned at me. "Not any longer than I have to."

I gave him the address, and JD dropped the car into gear

and mashed the pedal. The four-banger buzzed. It didn't *roar*. It didn't *growl*. It didn't *snarl*. It buzzed.

"No loaner?"

"They were out of loaners. I have to settle for this until my car comes in. They're doing a dealer swap from Texas."

The rental car smelled like cheap plastic, air freshener, and the vague remnants of cigarette smoke that had soaked into the cloth seats. It was a far cry from a convertible Porsche, but with the windows rolled down and a little bit of imagination, you could pretend.

After racking up a considerable amount of abuse, Jack's Miami Blue 911 Turbo had been written off as a total loss. It went to that great car lot in the sky. Probably to be resurrected with a salvage title and sold to some poor unsuspecting victim on the internet, looking to buy their dream car.

I don't think Jack was too broken up about it. He liked shiny new things, and it was a fitting excuse for a new car.

The wind tousled his hair as we drove to *Whispering Heights*. It was an older neighborhood full of French colonial homes with verandas, pastel siding, and plenty of white picket fences. It wasn't *Stingray Bay* or the *Platinum Dunes Estates*, but it was nice. Twenty years ago, you could have bought into the neighborhood for a steal. Now the price of entry would put a serious dent in your pocketbook.

The neighborhood was famous for its annual display of Christmas lights. Residents spared no expense putting on the finest displays, all competing for the grand prize of $500 —though it wasn't about the money. Most residents spent orders of magnitude more than that on decorations. It was the prestige and bragging rights that residents coveted.

Esther Murray could brag more than anyone else. She was the reigning champion and had more titles than any other resident. People drove from all over the Keys just to cruise through the neighborhood during the holiday season. Each year, Esther's works of illumination were featured in the paper and on the news. She carried herself with the pride and swagger of an Olympic gold medalist.

But apparently, not everyone was so enamored with her creations.

Of course, she carefully navigated the homeowners' association rules against back-to-back winners by significantly changing the displays each year.

During the day, access to *Whispering Heights* wasn't a problem. At night, during the holidays, forget about it.

Every home in the neighborhood had to be lit up during the season. The HOA found creative ways to discipline those who failed to comply by using an extraordinary amount of social pressure, combined with what would best be described as harassment during the rest of the year. Put your garbage out too soon?—a letter from the homeowners' association. The porch light went out?—a letter from the homeowners' association. Paint peeling on the picket fence? —a letter from the homeowners' association, along with the threat of fines.

The people on the board were little tyrants. These people seriously didn't have anything better to do than to butt into each other's business.

We pulled to the curb at Pintail Park and hopped out of the car. The problem was obvious.

Every other house on the street was perfectly intact. But in its current state, Esther's handiwork wasn't going to win any prizes this year.

2

Someone had plowed through the yard, leaving two deep ruts in the grass that rivaled the Grand Canyon. The reindeer were victims of the drive-by, and a string of lights had been yanked from the bushes.

We made our way up the walkway and climbed the steps to the veranda. Before I could knock on the door, a yappy-dog went ape-shit. There was no need, but I knocked anyway.

A woman called through the door a few moments later. "Who is it?"

I flashed my badge. "Coconut County."

She pulled open the door, cradling an aggressive chihuahua under one arm like a football. The dog snarled and barked incessantly, its pearly teeth on full display.

Esther took a deep breath. "It took you long enough."

"The department gets pretty busy this time of year," I said. "We came as soon as we got the call."

Her disapproving eyes looked us up and down. JD looked like a beach bum—long, mostly blond hair, Hawaiian shirt, checkered Vans.

Esther Murray was in her mid 60s with stark white hair in a stylish short cut, a square face, and narrow brown eyes.

"When did this happen?" I asked.

"It was around 3 AM. I heard the rumble of an engine, and little Leonidas here went crazy," she said, stroking his head.

The little guy finally calmed down, but still growled from time to time.

"Did you happen to see who did this?"

"No. By the time I got to the window, they were long gone. I'm just heartbroken over it," she said, sagging. "I worked so hard on this display. It's just not fair. My daughter, Arielle, would have been so proud of this. She used to help me with the decorations every year. I feel like it's all I have left of her."

Esther put her hand over her chest and her eyes brimmed. She wasn't putting on an act, but she might have been playing it up just a tad.

"I'm very sorry for your loss," I said.

"I do hope you find the people responsible for this heinous crime against humanity."

"We will do our best," I assured.

She leaned in and whispered, "I don't think this was a random occurrence. You can bet your bottom dollar this was one of my competitors."

"What makes you so sure?"

She looked almost offended. Esther stood tall and lifted her nose in the air. "In case you are unaware, I am the reigning champion. I'm clearly a high-profile target, and this year's decorations were better than anything I have done previously. I'm all but guaranteed to win. At least, I was. I don't know if I can salvage this," she said in a dramatic exhale. "There are only a few days left before the judging."

"I'm sure a resourceful woman such as yourself will be able to pull something together."

She regarded me carefully for a moment, processing the compliment. She puffed up slightly. "I certainly will. You watch. I'm still going to win this competition. Nothing is going to keep me down."

"That's the spirit."

She whispered again. "But you need to look into my neighbor."

"Your neighbor?"

"Carol Anderson," she said, souring her face. "That witch will do anything to beat me. But it's not going to happen." She paused and pointed across the street, one door down. "She lives right there. I think you need to have a word with her."

"We'll speak with her," I said, trying to placate the woman.

An older gentleman appeared in the foyer behind Esther.

"Coconut County finally arrived," Esther called over her shoulder.

"That's good. Because I'm sick of hearing about it."

Esther's face crinkled. "This is my husband, Ben."

He was late 60s with a narrow frame, gray hair, and sun-weathered skin. He had a slight hunch in his back. "I hope you catch the bastard who did this. Those lights were expensive. And they broke the sprinkler system. I had to shut the water off."

He had a narrow face, a bulbous nose, and steely blue eyes. His skin was red from a touch of rosacea and a few broken capillaries.

"I suppose you didn't see anything either?" I asked.

He shook his head. "They're lucky I didn't see them do it. They'd have to deal with me."

Esther rolled her eyes.

"If they come back, call the department right away," I said. "Don't take matters into your own hands."

Esther scoffed. "I called the department at 3:30 AM this morning. And you guys are just now showing up. What kind of response time is that? I mean, it's a good thing neither one of us was in real danger. I'd hate to see how you respond to a home invasion or something serious."

"Again, I'm sorry for the delay, ma'am. I'm sure your call was prioritized behind some of the more urgent cases."

She didn't like that. "Well, excuse me, but I happen to think this is an urgent case that demands attention. I'm an upstanding member of this community, I pay my taxes, and I vote."

"I pay the taxes," Ben muttered before walking away. He had enough of the conversation.

"I can assure you. We will devote the appropriate resources to solving this case."

"What does that mean? What do you deem appropriate?"

"Do you happen to have any security cameras?"

"No. I have lived in this house for 30 years, and this neighborhood never needed security cameras until recently."

"We'll check with the neighbors and see if anyone has a video doorbell. Maybe somebody saw something."

An annoyed look tensed her face. "Aren't you going to get the forensic investigators out here? Take molds of the tire tracks? That kind of thing?"

I exchanged a subtle glance with JD.

"Oh, right. This isn't a priority," she snarked.

"I can assure you—"

"I know, I know. You'll devote the appropriate resources." Esther frowned. "You tell that sheriff of yours that if he wants my support in the next election, he better damn sure give this case attention. I don't want this to end up in the unsolved files."

3

"I don't think Esther's going to be winning jack shit this year," a man said with an almost imperceptible grin on his face.

Stephen Bradford was an average guy in his mid 40s. He had a few lines around the eyes and his forehead. There was a touch of gray in his stubble and the sides of his brown hair. His droopy brown eyes gave him a lazy look. Not disheveled, just a little rough around the edges. He swept the street by the curb in front of his house. But he was really outside just to get a look at the damage and see what we were all about.

He lived directly across the street from Esther, and we encountered him as we returned to the rental car at the curb.

I flashed my badge and made introductions. "I don't suppose you happened to see anything last night?"

"I'm guessing this happened after midnight."

I nodded.

"I was out like a light at midnight. Slept solid. Didn't hear anything."

"Esther seems to think that maybe a competitor is responsible."

Stephen shrugged. "Don't look at me." He motioned to his yard. "I don't stand a chance. I just put up a few lights and call it a day so the HOA doesn't get on my ass."

He leaned in and muttered, cupping his hand to his mouth. "Between you and me, I'm over this shit. Every year we gotta deal with all these assholes driving through here to look at the lights. You know, sometimes it takes me 40 minutes to get out of my driveway and down the street. It's insane."

"What about Carol Anderson?" I asked. "It sounded like they aren't best friends."

Steve chuckled. "Those two women hate each other. That is a fight you do not want to get in the middle of."

"You think she's capable of this kind of vandalism?"

Steve frowned and shook his head. "She's a 65-year-old lady. She's not going to hop into a car and trench somebody's yard."

I shrugged. "Maybe. People do strange things."

Stephen thought about it for a moment. "You know, maybe. I wouldn't put anything past these women. When their claws come out, forget about it." He looked around to make sure no one was out on the street. "I know Carol wants to beat Esther. That's all she's been talking about this year. And last year. And the year before that." He paused. "To be honest, I hope Esther loses. I'm so sick of her smug attitude. If you hadn't noticed, she's got a high opinion of herself and her *artistic* skills," he mocked.

"She had a slightly abrasive quality," JD said, understating the situation.

"And that goddamn yappy-dog. That thing barks incessantly. Every time it sees me—*yap, yap, yap,*" he said, mimicking the barking dog with his hand. "Dogs love me, except for that one. Never had a dog snarl at me like that. Every time. And she lets it run over here to crap in my yard, then doesn't pick it up. She denies the crap belongs to her dog. *'That's too big for Leonidas,'*" he said, mimicking her.

"I take it you're not a fan of Mrs. Murray," I said.

Stephen looked at me flatly. He raised his hands innocently. "Hey, I get along with everybody."

"Except the dog."

"People. I get along with people. It just happens that Esther has a slightly difficult personality."

"And where were you last night?" I asked, even though he'd already said.

"Like I told you, I was inside sleeping at the time of the incident."

"If you didn't see it, how would you know what time it happened?"

"Like I said, it must have happened during the night. Sometime between midnight and 7 AM. The display was fine when I went to bed, and when I came out this morning..." He motioned across the street. "Well, you can see."

JD and I stared at him for a moment.

A nervous chuckle escaped his lips. "Look, I didn't get in my car in the middle of the night and drive through her yard, if that's what you're wondering. You want to take a look?"

"If you don't mind."

He scoffed. "Seriously?"

"You offered."

He sighed. "Follow me."

He walked up his driveway, and we trailed behind him. There were trash bags at the curb and empty boxes for an Eptex 3500 XT printer and a 65" OLED SG TV.

"Looks like Christmas came early," I said.

"Santa's gotta have something to open, right?"

He led us up to the back of a black Honda Civic. It was a late model with nice rims, 16-inch tires, and an aero kit. Pretty sporty for what it was. The tread was good on the tires, and there were no signs of dirt or debris. No blades of grass, no speckles of mud on the mudguards. Not the kind of car you'd use to jump the curb and go cross country on someone's lawn.

I figured the perpetrators drove a truck or SUV with higher clearance. "Is this the only vehicle you own?"

"I have a truck in the garage. Want to see it too?"

4

Stephen opened the driver's door and clicked the garage opener that hung from the sun visor of the Civic. The garage rumbled to life and retracted. Inside was a red Toyota truck. It was older, and a little weathered—an all-purpose utility vehicle.

We inspected the tires, and again there were no signs of mud or grass. But a smart criminal would hose the vehicle down after the joyride.

"Satisfied?" Stephen asked.

"For now."

Another annoyed chuckle escaped his lips. "I can appreciate your thoroughness and dedication, but you guys are treating this like a homicide."

I exchanged a glance with JD.

"That's our usual beat," I said.

Steve's face crinkled. "So why are you working on this?"

I smiled. "Luck of the draw."

Steve gave a nod of understanding.

"You wouldn't happen to have a video doorbell or a security cam, would you?"

"Sorry."

I snapped photos of the tire tread on both vehicles before walking back down the driveway. I dug into my pocket and gave Steve my card. "If you hear anything or can think of additional details, give me a call."

He gave us both a mock salute, "Yes, sir."

We walked next door to Carol Anderson's house and strolled the walkway to the veranda. In the daylight, it was hard to truly appreciate the work that had gone into the lighting arrangement. But I could tell that Carol Anderson had spared no expense in decorating her home.

The white columns of the pastel blue house were wrapped solid with red and white lights to look like candy canes. The palm trees and hedgerows were covered with lights. All the windows were rimmed with lights and LED icicles hung from cornices. The terrace above the veranda was full of elves and giant boxes of presents. Santa and his reindeer were on the roof, ready to deliver the goods. Nothing was left undecorated.

Was it a winning setup?

I'd have to see it at night. But it made the string of lights I hung around the *Avventura* look dismal.

I banged on the door, and Carol Anderson opened a few minutes later after I identified myself.

She had chocolate brown hair that hung just past her chin, with a few highlights. Her gray roots needed a touchup. She had blue eyes and flawless makeup and was a little on the frumpy side.

"I think it's just terrible what happened," she said before I could even ask a question. "I mean, who would do such a thing?"

"That's what we're here to find out," I said.

"You know, this neighborhood is just not what it used to be."

"So I'm told. Did you see or hear anything last night?"

"No. And it's just frightening to me that something like that could happen and I would sleep right through it." She frowned in an exaggerated way. "And I feel so bad for Esther. I know how hard she works on these displays."

She tried to sound sincere, but it was all an act.

She continued, "I guess she'll just have to settle for not placing this year."

"I don't know. Don't be so quick to count her out. She seems pretty determined."

Carol's face reddened slightly. "Well, I don't see how she can possibly salvage it in time. But if anyone can, it's Esther."

"You have a beautiful home and a wonderful display."

"Why thank you," she said with a smile. "Fingers crossed that I place this year."

"I have no doubt that you will. From what I understand, you placed second last year, and the year before that, and the year before that."

She looked a little surprised at my revelation and a little offended. She wasn't fond of second place. "You do your homework, Deputy. Surely you don't think I had something to do with this," she said, holding her hand to her chest innocently.

"Right now, we're just trying to get a sense of the dynamic. I understand you and Esther aren't the best of friends."

"No, we're not. But it wasn't always that way. We were very close at one point in time. I might even go so far as to say she was my best friend."

"What happened?"

Carol shrugged. "I don't know. People change. People come into your life for a reason, and then they go."

"It seems like she is still in your life."

"Only because she lives across the street." She sighed and frowned. "I tried to reach out and repair our friendship, but she wouldn't have any of it." Carol smiled. "But you don't want to hear the boring details of my life, do you?"

"Doesn't sound boring at all."

"I'd love to be of assistance, but I'm afraid I have nothing to add."

I got the impression that she didn't like talking to us. Most people don't like talking to cops unless they need them for something.

"You live alone, Mrs. Anderson?"

"I do. Sadly, Bernard passed a few years ago."

"My condolences."

"Thank you. It's been difficult, but I've managed. This time of year is always the hardest, as you can imagine."

"I can."

"But I have my daughter to get me through the difficult times."

A car pulled to the curb just then, and a young woman in her mid 30s got out. She stared at us with curious eyes. Blonde hair hung to her shoulders, and I could see the resemblance to Carol right away. She pushed through the gate of the picket fence and strolled the walkway to the veranda.

"Deputies, this is my daughter, Paige Anderson. She lives just a few blocks over on Nightingale."

We made introductions.

Paige had blue eyes, thin lips, and a concerned look on her face. She had the same build as her mother, but slightly less frumpy. "What's going on?"

"These deputies are here inquiring about the vandalism."

"Vandalism?" she said with wide eyes.

Carol pointed across the street.

Paige gasped. "Oh my God. I didn't even notice when I pulled up."

"It's just terrible," Carol said.

"Who would do something like this?" Paige asked.

"That's what these deputies trying to find out," Carol said.

"I guess it's anyone's ballgame this year," Paige commented.

"It would appear that way," I replied.

"Do you have any leads?" Paige asked.

"Not at this time."

Paige drove a beige Toyota Camry. I planned on taking a closer look before we left, but it didn't look like the type of vehicle you'd go off-roading in.

I asked Carol what kind of car she drove.

"I have a Lexus SUV. Why?" she asked with a knitted brow.

"Do you mind if we take a look at it?"

"What on earth for?"

"No, mother. Do not let them start snooping around your property," Paige glared at us. "Why are you harassing my mother like this?"

"Nobody is harassing anybody. We're just asking questions."

"I've got nothing to hide," she assured. "If they want to look at my car, they can look at my car."

"I'm sure some drunk asshole drove through in the middle of the night and decided to take a detour through Esther's yard," Paige said. "It's probably nothing more than that."

My car is right this way if you'd like to inspect it. She marched down the steps, cut across the lawn to the driveway, and we followed. Her black SUV was parked near the back door, and we took a moment to survey the vehicle, checking the tires and looking for any damage to the front bumper.

What we found was interesting.

5

There was dirt and gravel in the tread of the rear tires. Mud speckled the lower rear quadrant, along with a few blades of grass. Carol's vehicle had been off-road recently.

It raised questions.

"Care to explain this?" I said, pointing to the muddy tread.

"Explain what?" Carol asked with a crinkled face. She squinted and surveyed the tires. She shook her head dismissively. "That's nothing. I parked in the grass lot the other day just after the rains."

"Where at?"

"Overflow parking for the ballgame."

"What ballgame?"

"The 'Cudas.'"

"Who won?" I knew who won.

Her face tightened, and she put her hands on her hips. "Who do you think won? The 'Cudas'!"

"Mom, stop talking to them," Paige demanded.

"You can't possibly think I have some involvement in this?" Carol said. "That's utterly ridiculous."

"Just doing our due diligence, ma'am."

"Well, do it somewhere else," Paige said. "This is insulting."

I snapped photographs of the tire tread and dirt.

"I'm calling an attorney," Paige said.

"Paige, it's not a big deal," Carol said calmly. "Let them do what they need to do. I know I'm innocent. And if these deputies are worth their salt, they will discover that." Carol looked at me. "Can't you take some kind of dirt sample from the tire and match it against the dirt from Esther's yard? They do that kind of thing on TV all the time."

I'd been a little hesitant to get the forensic team involved in this. It was Christmas lights. It wasn't like somebody died. But I decided to call the department and get the unit out for good measure.

They arrived shortly and took samples of the dirt and grass from Carol's car as well as Esther's yard. They photographed the damage and the ruts in the yard and took impressions of the tire tracks.

At a glance, the tread pattern matched Carol's vehicle. But it was a common tire on trucks and SUVs. The tread wasn't even close to a match on Paige's Camry.

"Does anyone else have access to your vehicle, Mrs. Anderson?" I asked.

"No."

"No one? Not even your daughter?"

"No. I am the only person who drives that car. I'm the only one with a key. And I can assure you, my car has not been through Esther's yard."

By this time, Paris Delaney and her news crew were on the scene. The cameraman grabbed B-roll footage of the investigators in Esther's yard. I didn't think it was sensational enough for her, but it must have been a slow news day.

A small crowd of curious neighbors gathered around. Gossip and speculation swirled.

Paige's angry eyes glared at me. "What are you going to do, arrest my mom?"

"The investigators will take the evidence back to the lab and analyze it more thoroughly," I said. "Then we will make a determination."

"Then what?" she asked, exasperated.

I shrugged. "Depends on the results. We'll be in touch."

Paige's eyes burned into me.

I wasn't inclined to haul Carol down to the station until the lab had made a determination. I figured she wasn't going to skip town. She was an easy person to find.

Stephen Bradford leaned against his broom handle, watching the spectacle with a sly grin. We crossed paths as we walked back to the rental car. "Never a dull moment around here. This is First Class, Grade-A entertainment. The only thing better would be to see those two old biddies in a cage fight. I'd pay top dollar for that."

"Deputy Wild," Paris shouted. She rushed toward me along with her crew. Soon, the camera lens focused on me. "What can you tell us about the incident?"

"Vandals destroyed a holiday display."

"I can see that," she replied, trying to mask her annoyance. "Do you have a suspect?"

"We have a few persons of interest," I said with a smirk.

I climbed into the rental, leaving Paris somewhat frustrated by my lack of response. She spun around and faced the camera to finish the segment. I had no doubt she would hound Carol for a statement.

We drove back to the station to fill out reports. It wasn't long before Paris buzzed my phone. She said, "This is a little beneath you, isn't it?"

"Lights in the Heights is a Christmas tradition. This kind of vandalism is an attack on the Holiday spirit, American values, and our very way of life."

"Spare me. Why are you two working the case?"

"Favor to the sheriff."

"There has to be something more. Drugs, weapons, organized crime?" She paused. "I know. The two women are crime bosses in the middle of a turf war."

I chuckled. "Something like that. I promise I'll let you know if anything develops."

"What about Norah Bailey?"

"Who's Norah Bailey?"

6

"Oh, am I supposed to do your job for you now, Deputy?" Paris asked in a sassy tone.

I stifled a groan. "What do you know?"

"I know that she's a strong competitor for this year's prize. At least, that's the word on the street. Maybe you should have a chat with her."

"Maybe."

"But you're probably right to focus your attention on Carol Anderson. I mean, the tire tread is a match, isn't it?"

"We'll know more when the lab results come back."

"There is no love lost between those two women, let me tell you."

"That's what I gathered."

"Nobody has surveillance?"

"Not in the immediate vicinity."

"You know, I'm going to be really amused if the great Tyson Wild gets stumped by this case."

"I am not going to get stumped by this case."

"Care to put your money where your mouth is?"

"What do you have in mind?"

I could almost hear her devious smile. "I've got a lot of things in mind."

"I solve this case, you tell me who your source is inside the department," I said.

"No can do, Deputy. Professional ethics."

I scoffed.

"I may be a lot of things, but I keep to my word."

I couldn't argue with that. She was ambitious, driven, and perhaps a little self-centered, but she wasn't a *bad* person.

"Tell you what, if you fail to solve the case, you buy me dinner and drinks."

"And if I solve the case?"

"I buy you dinner and drinks."

"Seems like you win either way."

"Aren't we cocky?" she snarked.

"If I recall correctly, you already owe me."

She thought for a moment. "You're right. I do. I'm sure I can think of a few ways to make it up to you."

"I'm sure."

"Do we have a deal?"

"I'll give it consideration."

"What's the matter, Deputy? Getting cold feet? Doubting your ability?"

"Taunting me is not going to work."

She sighed. "Okay. We'll keep it simple. $100."

"Deal."

Challenge accepted.

"Gotta go. Talk to you later, loser." She ended the call, and I dialed Isabella, my handler at *Cobra Company*.

I hated to call in a favor on a simple thing like Christmas lights, but Paris had made this a question of professional reputation. No way was I gonna let this investigation go unsolved.

"I need you to do me a favor," I said. "Don't laugh."

"This sounds interesting," Isabella replied, mildly intrigued.

Cobra Company was an off-the-books private agency with vast intelligence resources. They were the people the three-letter agencies called when they needed something done but didn't ever want it to be traced back to them. Plausible deniability.

I gave her Esther Murray's address and asked her to look up the cellular data in that area around the time of the incident. Perhaps the perpetrators were stupid enough to have their cell phones turned on as they were barreling through her yard.

"And why do you need this data?"

I cringed and gave her the details.

Isabella certainly had better things to do than to chase down small-time perpetrators of criminal mischief. Surprisingly, she was all about it. "That kinda stuff just pisses me off. You know, you try to have nice things, and somebody's gotta screw it up."

"So, you'll help?"

"I'll see what I can do."

"I appreciate you."

"I know," she sang back to me.

I ended the call and finished typing up my report. If this was the worst thing that happened in Coconut Key this Christmas, we would be in good shape.

But that was wishful thinking.

7

"This place totally sucks," Scarlett said.

"Maybe you should've thought about that before you did something stupid," Jack chided.

She wore a navy blue ball cap pulled low. Dark sunglasses shielded her eyes, even though we were indoors in the visiting area of the Coconut Key Addiction and Recovery Center.

Scarlett sat on a beige leather couch with her arms folded, pouting. She had decided to serve out her studio-imposed mandatory rehab here on the island. She figured there would be fewer paparazzi than in Los Angeles, but when we arrived, there were several fans loitering around the parking lot, hoping to catch a glimpse of the rising star.

It was all for publicity purposes, trying to avoid the backlash from her accident, combined with the fact that the studio needed a completion bond on the film. The budget for *Ultra Mega 3* was already over $200 million, and the underwriter sure as hell wasn't going to sign off on production if the lead actor had a substance abuse problem.

Scarlett would do her stint. The insurance company would be happy. The studio would begin production on *Ultra Mega 3*, and Scarlett would, hopefully, continue her meteoric rise to fame and fortune. This would just be a speed bump.

"One drink," Scarlett said. "One drink! You have that before breakfast," she said, pointing at Jack. "I don't want to hear any more about this. I've heard enough."

"We just stopped by to say hello and see how you're doing," I said.

Scarlett smiled at me, her bottle-blonde hair tucked in a ponytail sprouting out the back of the cap. "Thank you, Tyson."

"How's it going so far?"

"The food here sucks. The beds are uncomfortable. But there are really cool people here, so I guess there's that. I mean, I think it was a little weird for them at first. Here's this *'movie star,'*" she mocked with air quotes, "showing up to rehab."

"I don't know if you qualify as a *'movie star'* just yet," JD snarked.

Scarlett huffed. "I starred in two box office #1 hits. I think that makes me a *'movie star.'*" She looked at me for support. "Doesn't it?"

"Technically, I think so."

"Just don't get too big for your britches," JD said.

She stuck her tongue out at him.

Hollywood shuts down over the holidays. It becomes a ghost town, and things don't get rolling again until mid-January. The plan was for Scarlett to do her time here, under the radar, spend the holiday with Jack, then head back to begin production.

JD looked at his watch. "I gotta roll. I'll be back tomorrow. You need me to bring you anything?"

"I'm good, thank you."

We stood up, and she gave us both hugs.

"The local news wants to do an interview," I said.

"No. Absolutely not. Are you kidding me? Look at me. I'm not talking to anybody like this."

"That's what I thought."

"Plus, all press requests have to go through my publicist. I can't say anything that's not scripted at this point."

"It's a gilded cage, isn't it?"

"You'd think the world would get bigger when you're famous. But it kind of gets smaller."

"Stay out of trouble," JD said as we left.

We pushed outside, and a fan approached JD. "Are you Jack Donovan?"

He looked at the guy curiously. "I could be."

"You're Scarlett Nicole's dad, right?"

"I could be."

The fan's eyes lit up, and his face filled with awe and wonder. "So you're responsible for the goddess."

Jack tried to stifle an eye roll. "Partially."

He extended his hand. "Dude, you're the man. Your daughter is so hot."

Jack wasn't sure whether or not to shake the guy's hand.

"You think you could do me a favor?"

Jack surveyed him curiously.

"Can you get me an autograph? I'd kill for a fucking autograph, man."

It wasn't long before the other fans swarmed JD and the paparazzi started snapping photos.

"Me too. Can you get me an autograph?" a girl asked.

Then another chimed in. "Please, me too!"

Jack surveyed the group. There were half a dozen fans gathered around, ranging from 15 to 25 years old.

Jack, the budding entrepreneur, asked, "How much are you willing to pay?"

"$40 bucks," the guy said.

I gave Jack a nudge with my elbow.

His face crinkled, then he relented and addressed the fans. "I'll ask her and see if she's willing. I know she adores her fans. She might even do it for free."

"That would be so awesome," the guy said. "We would be forever in your debt."

I waited outside while JD darted back into the rehab facility and found Scarlett.

The fans waited nervously with fingers crossed, anticipation filling their faces. They looked like the world would end if Scarlett said *no*.

8

J ack poked his head out the front door a few moments later and motioned the fans over. They crowded around the entrance, and the paparazzi rattled off camera flashes like machine-gun fire.

Jack told the fans to form a line, and Scarlett made a brief appearance at the doorway. She was greeted by shrieks of joy as excited fans bounced up and down. With a silver sharpie, she signed the covers of Blu-rays and autographed pictures that fans had printed from the internet. All at no charge.

Jack controlled the crowd well, moving the show along. The autograph session only lasted a few minutes. The fans were overjoyed, in awe of their new prized possessions.

It was good for Scarlett, too.

Afterward, Jack asked the fans to respect Scarlett's privacy, and give her space. The crowd dispersed. We left the rehab facility and drove across the island to the warehouse district for band practice.

I had booked *Wild Fury* for the New Year's Eve Ball on the strip. Oyster Avenue would be shut down and blocked off, allowing pedestrians full run of the street. A stage would be erected with giant speakers and scaffolding containing lights. Multiple bands were slated to play a free concert with *Wild Fury* headlining. It wouldn't be their biggest show yet, but it would be a hell of an event.

The guys rocked out their set a few times in the practice space. As usual, groupies filled the room, eager to get a free show. *Wild Fury* worked up a new song, *Behind the Eight Ball*. They cobbled together a rough version and ran through it a few times. Styxx usually wrote the lyrics, but Jack gave it a go this time. The song chronicled our recent escapades around a pool table and a run-in with some pretty surly dudes.

I liked it.

It had that *Wild Fury* magic, and with a little polish, I was sure it would be a permanent part of their repertoire.

The group had a pretty egalitarian way of writing music and splitting royalties. Any member of the band could bring a song to the group, and they'd work it up together. Before I came on as manager, royalties were split four ways. The guys decided to give me an equal share for my efforts, and that also meant I had equal say in the song selection. The band wouldn't put out anything that didn't get a thumbs up from everyone involved. The guys figured if there was a member that didn't love the song, there would be fans that wouldn't love it either.

The back end of the music business is a nightmare to navigate. It's every bit as bad as the movie industry, if not worse.

There are various individuals and entities that have rights to a song—the person who wrote it, the person who performed it, the person who recorded it, the person who distributed it, and the person who collected the publishing.

Performance rights organizations collected money from songs that were played on the radio or performed in live venues. After their cut, they passed the revenue back to whoever held the publishing rights, which may or may not have been the songwriter. Mechanical royalties from the popular streaming sites were collected by another organization. And yet another organization collected digital performance royalties like internet radio, synchronization rights from video platforms like YouTube and other sites.

It was a Byzantine nightmare of multiple low-paying revenue sources. Only top artists made real money in the music business. The majority of revenue for most indie bands came from merchandise sales—T-shirts, CDs, direct downloads, special limited-edition vinyl editions, and whatever else bands could think of. Modern musicians had to be entrepreneurs as well as musical geniuses.

It was my job to navigate the ins-and-outs of all of that. It was enough to make your head spin. And I had no real background in any of it.

After practice, we were all deciding on what bar to hit when Sheriff Daniels called. "Meet me down at the station. We've got a situation."

I groaned. "What is it this time? Don't tell me someone wrecked another Christmas decoration?"

"I'll tell you when you get here."

I told JD we were needed, and the band groaned. They'd get along just fine without us—though Jack wouldn't be there to pick up the tab as usual.

We hustled out of the practice studio, darted across the lot, and hopped into the rental car. Jack drove the little four-cylinder like a bat out of hell. It was no Porsche, and it certainly didn't corner like one. The engine buzzed, and there was an incessant rattle under the dash. The suspension was terrible. The car had a lot of body roll. Through the twists and turns, it was like a ship on the high seas.

We pulled into the parking lot at the station and hustled down the dock to join the sheriff onboard a Defender class patrol boat. We cast off the lines, and Daniels idled us out of the marina. He throttled up, bringing the boat on plane.

The sun had long since dipped below the horizon, and the moonlight glimmered on the inky swells as we crashed through the waves, spraying mists of saltwater. The engine howled, spitting a frothy white wake.

It didn't take long to come upon the *War Games*. The sleek superyacht had been out on a sunset cruise when things went awry.

9

"**A** guy went missing from a company Christmas party," Daniels said as we pulled to the swim platform of the superyacht.

"Maybe he left early," I joked.

Daniels shot me a look.

"Maybe he's banging a co-worker in a guest stateroom," JD added.

Daniels was equally unimpressed by his comment.

We tied off at the stern and boarded the 142' superyacht. It wasn't the biggest boat around Coconut Key, but the *Sun Trekker* was impressive with its angled lines and sculpted form.

There was a cellist playing Christmas classics as we climbed the steps to the aft deck. Waitstaff dashed about in formal attire, delivering drinks and hors d'oeuvres. The guests were all dressed in evening wear. I noticed a Marine Colonel in Dress Blues. There was an air of concern among the attendees, but they attempted to go about their business as if nothing was wrong.

We were greeted by a woman in her mid 30s with a svelte figure and golden-blonde hair that hung just above her shoulders. An expensive red evening gown hugged her petite form and displayed voluptuous mounds of cleavage that drew the eye to a sparkling diamond necklace. The jewels demanded a second glance.

She was a good-looking woman. No doubt about it.

A little lip-filler here and there and a few Botox injections in her forehead kept her face perfectly smooth. With a good facial and a flawless application of makeup—that she no doubt hired someone to do before the event—she looked pageant-worthy. "I'm Alexandria West. You must be Sheriff Daniels," she said, extending her hand.

The two shook, and Daniels introduced JD and me.

She gave us a curious glance. Neither of us looked like members of a special crimes unit.

The patter of rotor blades thumped the air overhead. Tango One scoured the seas along with the Coast Guard, searching for the missing passenger, Paul Brown.

"This is my partner and Chief Financial Officer, Jenson Ward."

We shook hands and made introductions. Jenson was early 40s, impeccably dressed in a *Di Fiore* suit, and had a touch of gray on the sides. He had enough wrinkles to make him look dignified. A strong brow, dark eyes, and a square jaw endeared him to the ladies—along with his fat bank account. He carried himself as a man of value, and the Rolex Oyster Perpetual added to that impression.

Alexandria introduced us to Linda Brown. She was shorter and not quite as attractive as Alexandria. Though, not many were. Alexandria had charm, grace, and an alluring quality. She was the bright star that all others revolved around— especially in her universe. She was rich, powerful, and capable.

Linda had dirty blonde hair that went just past her shoulders. Her brown eyes were red and puffy, and her face was tense with worry. She trembled slightly, blotting her eyes from time to time with a tissue.

"When was the last time you saw your husband?" Daniels asked.

"I can't be sure. We had gotten into a fight. He'd been drinking pretty heavily. He always gets a little obnoxious when he drinks. He got into an... *altercation* with one of his co-workers. I was fed up with the situation. He went one way. I went another. We both needed time to cool off."

"And you've already searched the entire boat?" Daniels asked. "You're sure he's not sleeping it off in a stateroom somewhere?"

Alexandria said, "We searched the entire boat three times. We looked in every nook and cranny. The staterooms, the crew quarters, the engine room. We can't find him anywhere."

"What was the fight about?" Daniels asked.

Linda hesitated.

"The fight was about the fact that Paul's banging my wife," an angry man shouted, standing nearby.

Alexandria forced a smile.

Kevin Gardner's wife tried to calm him down. "Honey..."

"Don't honey me!" Kevin said with a scowl.

His wife groaned and shook her head.

Tensions were running high. Kevin's face was beet red, and he looked like he was about to explode.

"Okay," Daniels said in a stern tone. "Everybody needs to calm down."

"This is Kevin Gardner," Alexandria said. "He's the husband of our valued employee Kim." Alexandria tried her best to diffuse the situation.

Kevin was 6'1", 200 pounds, with peanut brown hair, cornflower blue eyes, and a slightly round face. Average features. His wife, Kim, was out of his league. I wouldn't go so far as to call her a stunner. But she had *qualities*. She'd settled. And by the sound of things, she was pursuing other options.

"The bastard's lucky he disappeared, or I'd have made him disappear," Kevin slurred.

"Maybe you did," Daniels said, staring at the man.

Kevin suddenly realized he was in the hot seat and raised his hands innocently. "I didn't do nothing."

"The hell you didn't. You sucker-punched my husband," Linda snapped.

"Your husband's sticking it to my wife. Wake up, Lady!"

"You're so full of it, Kevin," Kim snapped. "Nobody is sticking it to me. And certainly not you tonight."

Kevin raised his hands and wiggled them. "Oooh, big threat! It's not like I'm getting any, anyway."

Kim groaned again.

"Let me get this straight," Daniels interrupted. "You assaulted Paul Brown. Then he disappeared."

Kevin swallowed hard. "The two things are completely unrelated."

"I'll need to have a word with you all individually," Daniels said, sweeping his finger at everyone in the immediate vicinity. "The first thing we need to do is search every inch of this boat one more time, just to make sure." His attention focused on Linda. "Do you have a recent picture of Paul?"

She nodded and scrolled through the images on her phone. She found a picture of Paul and showed it to us. We all took a good, long look.

Paul had short dark hair, brown eyes, a square face, a long nose, and dark stubble, even after he had just shaved. He was late 30s and not much of a looker, though reasonably fit. He was a match for Linda, but Kim Gardner was definitely out of his league. He obviously had some kind of mojo, if Kevin's Gardner suspicions were correct. Some guys just have an innate charm.

I asked Linda, "Do you recall where Paul was the last time you saw him?"

She thought for a moment. "After the fight was broken up, Paul got another drink. He talked with another co-worker for a moment, then I recall him heading down the forward passage toward the day head."

"Who broke up the fight?" I asked.

"I did, along with Jenson and another gentleman," the Marine Colonel said as he stepped to us. He looked around and pointed out the other man who assisted.

"This is Colonel McFarlane," Alexandria said. "And the gentleman he just pointed to is Tom Byrd." She called to Tom and motioned him over, then made introductions.

Byrd was a big guy—late 30s, 6'3", 240 pounds. The physique of a lineman. He had a square jaw, brown eyes, and short, dark hair. His chin was beginning to sag. I figured him for a college ball player back in the day. He could easily break up a fight or finish one.

The colonel was carved of granite. He had a lined face, focused olive eyes, and angled brows—resting war face. His hair was high and tight, and he was all squared away.

He introduced us to Dale Doyle, Deputy Director of Systems Command. He was a senior civilian official.

"What exactly does your company do, Mrs. West?" I asked.

"Ms. West," she corrected, with a flirty glimmer in her eyes.

10

"**W**est-Tek *Advanced Integrated Systems and Performance*," Alexandria said.

"That's a mouthful," I said.

Alexandria chuckled. "It is, indeed."

"I'm still not exactly sure what you do."

"Come with me, Deputy, and I will explain as we look once again for Paul."

I followed her into the salon and may or may not have observed her enticing backside. Paul certainly wasn't hiding under her dress, but I might have to look just to be certain.

She strutted with confidence through her domain.

The deputies fanned out to search the ship.

The salon was spacious and well-appointed. The large windows offered stunning views during the day. There was a lounge area, a full bar, and a formal dining area near the forward bulkhead.

I surveyed the compartment and the guests as we passed through.

"West-Tek is a cutting-edge technology company connecting platforms and integrating systems," Alexandria said. "We constantly push the boundaries of science and technology, serving some of the most important and challenging missions in the world. With proprietary software and advanced artificial intelligence algorithms, we serve as a capability multiplier, optimizing performance, facilitating human and machine interaction. With an unwavering commitment to our customers and a singular purpose, West-Tek is driving innovation, creating products and services that will change the world."

It was a well-rehearsed speech. One she'd said many times, stuffed full of industry buzzwords.

I still didn't know exactly what her company did, but I had a good idea. Anytime somebody speaks about their work in such opaque language, it can only mean one thing. Given the name of the yacht and the presence of the Marine Colonel, it didn't take a rocket scientist to figure it out.

"Is this your boat?" I asked as we moved through the forward passage, past the central staircase to the VIP stateroom. The boat shared a similar layout to the *Avventura*.

"It belongs to the company. But I own the company," she said with a wink.

She opened the hatch and pushed into the full-beam stateroom. There was a queen berth with his-and-hers hanging lockers, a lounge area, an office area with a desk, and an en suite with his-and-hers sinks and a shower. The porcelain tile on the deck looked like bleached hardwoods. A steamer trunk sat at the foot of the bed. My previous experience with steamer trunks made me want to look inside. "Mind if I take a look?"

Alexandria arched an eyebrow at me. "You think Paul's in the trunk?"

"Leave no stone unturned."

She smiled. "Knock yourself out."

I unlatched the trunk and lifted the lid. There were piles of neatly folded linens inside. I closed the lid and latched it.

"Is this your personal stateroom?"

"When I stay aboard, yes."

"How often do you stay aboard?"

"More so, recently. There's something about living on the water."

"I agree."

Satisfied that Paul wasn't in the compartment, we stepped out of the VIP stateroom. Alexandria flipped off the light and pulled the hatch shut behind us.

Erickson and Faulkner were on the sky deck, and Daniels mingled with the crowd, asking questions, getting various points of view on the events.

Alexandria showed us the galley and food storage compartment, then led us below deck, where she gave us a tour of the additional guest rooms, crew quarters, and engine room.

After a thorough search, we rejoined the others on the aft deck.

Faulkner shook his head. "He's not here."

11

"**K**evin is full of shit," Kim said when I asked her about the accusations. "I may flirt with Paul from time to time, but that's it. There's nothing going on between us. We're co-workers, and it's against office policy."

Just because something was against office policy didn't mean it didn't happen.

I looked deep into her eyes, trying to assess the situation. I didn't note any obvious signs of deception. She maintained eye contact. She didn't fidget nervously, and she didn't have any odd twitches.

"Why does Kevin suspect an affair?"

"I will often have communications with Paul on the weekends about work. We have some inside jokes between us. Kevin is insecure and overly protective."

"When was the last time you saw Paul?"

"Just after the fight. The colonel and Tom pulled them apart, and like Alexandria said, the last time I saw him, he was heading toward the day head."

"What did Kevin do after the fight?"

"Colonel McFarlane pulled him onto the aft deck and tried to calm him down. Kevin wasn't about to give the colonel shit."

"What does your husband do for a living?"

Kim scoffed. "Are you kidding me? He's a professional sponge."

"So he's unemployed."

"At the moment. And that moment has gone on for quite a long time."

The wait staff continued to weave through the crowd with drinks and hors d'oeuvres, and the cellist still played music.

Kim's face twisted with worry. "What do you think the odds are that they'll find him if he fell overboard?"

I shrugged.

"He was pretty drunk. I'm not sure how good of a swimmer he is."

I thanked her for her cooperation, then rejoined JD. He'd been speaking with Linda Brown. "What's her thoughts on the affair?"

JD shrugged. "I think she's a little suspicious. She said that Paul does spend a lot of time with Kim on work-related projects. But she's got no conclusive proof, and Paul always denied any wrongdoing."

"What about Kevin? Can anybody account for his whereabouts during the time of Paul's disappearance?"

"By all accounts, he remained on the aft deck and in the salon," JD said.

I found Colonel McFarlane and asked him a few more questions.

"I talked to Kevin for quite a bit," the colonel said. "He finally settled down."

"Did you have eyes on him the entire time?"

"Not the entire time. But I'm pretty sure he was in this general area. You think he may have had a hand in helping Mr. Brown overboard?"

"It's a distinct possibility," I said.

"What is your relationship to West-Tek?"

A sly smirk curled on his hard face. "Now, Deputy, you know better than to ask questions like that."

"You're Systems Command," I said.

"I am."

"Let me guess, West-Tek is providing equipment?"

"Again, Deputy, I'm not going to comment on current or pending contracts."

His answers told me everything I needed to know.

It didn't really matter, anyway. It wasn't relevant to the situation.

"How well do you know Paul?"

"He's one of the employees at West-Tek that I deal with on occasion."

"Nice guy?"

"During business hours. He certainly doesn't seem to handle his liquor well. In my eyes, that's a weakness. He's not sleeping with my wife, so I have no problem with the gentleman."

"Do you have any intel about his extracurricular activities?"

The colonel chuckled. "No, I don't, Deputy. I may have observed some lingering glances between the two and a few provocative comments. But nothing more than harmless cocktail party flirtations."

I thanked him and rejoined JD and Sheriff Daniels.

"If you ask me, the dipshit put back a few too many and stumbled over the railing," JD said.

"Maybe it's that simple," I said. "Maybe it's not."

"You're suspicious by nature," JD said.

"I'm suspicious by nature for a reason."

"Kevin Gardner denies any involvement, and everybody I talked to said he was on the aft deck or in the salon," Daniels said.

"He certainly had a motive to push Paul overboard," I muttered.

"His wife did, too."

I left JD and the sheriff and found Alexandria. She was talking to a group of gentlemen. "Excuse me while I borrow her for a moment."

I ushered her aside. "I just have a few more questions for you."

"Certainly. I'm an open book. I consider my employees family. I'm just devastated over this. And Paul was a key member of my team."

"Can you account for Linda Brown's whereabouts during the time of Paul's disappearance?"

She looked a little surprised. "You don't think foul play was involved, do you?"

"I've learned not to rule anything out."

"I had a few words in private with Paul after the incident. I try to stay out of my employees' lives, but obviously, a scenario like this affects the entire company. I'm sure you figured out by now there are some very important people here at this gathering, and Paul's actions reflect negatively on the organization as a whole. If I can't control my employees and their spouses, it calls into question my leadership capabilities. If my leadership is questioned, other aspects may be questioned, such as my ability to deliver on time and as promised. Perception and image are everything. And as they say, it takes a lifetime to build a reputation and an instant to lose it."

"Where were you when you had your chat with Paul?"

"By the day head. I had gone back to my stateroom to change my dress."

"You always do multiple outfit changes during an event?" I asked.

She smiled. "I was clumsy and spilled red wine on my gown. Fortunately, I had other options."

"It's a beautiful option, I must say."

"Thank you, Deputy," she said with a grin.

The dress looked great. It would have looked even better on the deck.

"And that was the last time you saw Paul?"

"Yes. We had our brief chat, then he slipped into the day head, and I returned to my guests."

She looked across the salon at Kevin Gardner. "Believe me, I had a few choice words for Kim Gardner as well. And I can tell you, Kevin Gardner is not getting invited back to next year's Christmas party." Alexandria paused. "How long will you continue to search for Paul?"

"It really depends. 3 to 5 days. Hopefully, he turns up before then, alive and well."

"Amen."

"What about Paul's mental state?"

"You mean, was he depressed?"

I nodded.

"No. I mean, I don't think so. But you never know what someone is dealing with, do you?"

I agreed.

"I don't think the altercation with Kevin was a trigger for him to throw himself off the boat if that's what you're getting at."

"You believe they were having an affair?"

12

"Is there a point in speculating?" Alexandria said. "Kevin Gardner thinks they were, and that seems to be motive enough."

"True."

The sound of rotor blades still thumped in the distance as helicopters searched the grid.

"I guess we should turn this ship around and head back to the island."

I nodded.

"This is not how I had planned the evening." Alexandria sighed. "I'll inform the captain."

"We need to take a statement from everybody, including the wait staff, before anyone departs the vessel."

"I don't see a problem with that. I pray to God your people find Paul safe and sound. But if there was foul play involved, you'd better nail the bastard to the wall. Paul was instrumental in our most recent deal."

"What deal was that?"

She smirked. "I can't discuss that."

"I understand."

I returned to the aft deck and joined Sheriff Daniels, JD, and the deputies.

"Learn anything interesting?" Daniels asked.

"Not really."

There were roughly 50 guests aboard the boat, and no one had seen anything. Most of the activity was either on the aft deck, the salon, or the sky deck. It seemed hard to imagine that Paul could have fallen off the boat without anyone noticing or hearing a splash. But situational awareness declines for most people at cocktail parties.

The superyacht turned and headed back to Coconut Key.

After we'd taken statements and collected information, the guests dispersed. Linda Brown was a nervous wreck. A coworker made sure she got home all right.

At the time we left the marina at Sandpiper Point, Paul still hadn't been found. My optimism was quickly fading. There were plenty of people who'd survived the night at sea after falling overboard. But without a life preserver, the odds weren't in your favor. Every now and then, someone would find a bit of debris to cling to, keeping them afloat. Many were picked up by passing boaters. Shark attacks were rare but not unheard of. The ocean can be a scary place at night, alone in the void.

JD persuaded me that we needed to go to Oyster Avenue to blow off steam. It didn't take much convincing, and we ended up at *Red November*. It was a submarine-themed bar, made to somewhat resemble a Russian Typhoon class submarine. It was new, and we'd been there a few times before. The waitresses were cute, their costumes were skimpy, and the drinks were reasonably priced.

We had a few cocktails, took in the scenery, and speculated about the cases. On the way home, we took a detour through *Whispering Heights*. The traffic crawled along as spectators gawked at the displays. Esther's street was filled with red brake lights and exhaust fumes. To my surprise, she'd completely redone her decorations and incorporated the vandalism in the final artwork.

Esther had used the ruts in the yard to her advantage. Santa's sleigh crashed. The reindeer were discombobulated. Presents were scattered about the yard, along with empty beer bottles. Santa staggered out of the sleigh with a beer in his hand.

Passersby snapped photos. Some hopped out of their cars and posed with the drunken Santa. The modified decorations were a bonafide hit. I must say, it gave me a good chuckle as we passed by, and I appreciated Esther's ingenuity.

I could see what Stephen Bradford was complaining about. It took forever to get down the street. Once we made it out of the fray, JD headed back to *Diver Down* and dropped me off at the dock. I told him I'd catch up with him in the morning, and he zipped away in the little four-cylinder.

I hustled down the dock, took Buddy out for a walk, then settled in for the evening. I watched a little TV before nodding off and caught Paris Delaney commenting on the vandalism and Esther's new design. Apparently, the depiction was already causing controversy among some of the residents.

"I'm sorry, but this is sending the wrong message to our children," a resident said on camera.

"I think it's funny as hell," a man said with a beer in his hand.

Another resident said, "It's inappropriate."

"We'll keep you updated as the situation develops," Paris said, looking directly into the camera lens. "Live in Coconut Key, I'm Paris Delaney."

I should have known someone would complain. And I had no doubt that Carol Anderson was probably spearheading the campaign. I clicked off the TV and went to bed.

It seemed like I had just closed my eyes when the sheriff called. "I need you two to get over to Fort Dawson. We've got a problem."

13

The state park at Fort Oliver Dawson was placed on the National Register in '72 and designated a National Historic Landmark in '73. It was 50 acres of history. You could spend the day snorkeling off the pristine beaches, fishing from the jetties, or meandering through the ruins of the old fort.

The white sand was the ideal location for that beach wedding. The onsite cafe was the perfect compliment for the reception. If you fancied something more unique, you could tie the knot under the brick archways of the fort and dance the night away under the stars in the courtyard.

But we weren't here for a wedding reception.

The park was a popular destination for kids after hours. Fort Dawson closed at sundown, but it was easy to bypass the security gate. The gearing on the lever arm was broken, and it didn't take much to lift it up and drive through. You could park under the stars at a small bluff that overlooked the beach and jetties and try to get to third base. Maybe even slide into home.

Bo, the park ranger, was pretty good about running teens off —most of the time without a citation. But get a little mouthy, and you'd get hit with criminal trespass.

But tonight, I bet these kids would have preferred Bo stumbled across them.

The fire department doused the amber flames that crackled into the night sky, illuminating the parking area by the bluff. Smoke and steam billowed, and metal popped and pinged. The white car was charred to a crisp, covered in soot.

The occupants looked like lumps of coal. It was a gut-wrenching sight. The acrid stench of burning rubber, leather, and flesh filled the air. Red and blues from emergency vehicles flickered.

Brenda and her team arrived. Dietrich snapped photos, and forensics investigators eagerly awaited firefighters to get the blaze under control.

"Any idea what happened?" I asked Sheriff Daniels.

"The vehicle was on fire when he came upon it." He pointed to the park ranger.

The rear license plate was still partially visible. Daniels was able to get registration information. "Car is registered to Milton Bouchard. I called, and he said his son had taken the vehicle out tonight on a date. I'm assuming the driver is his son, Blake, and the passenger is his date."

I cringed. No parent ever wanted to get a call in the middle of the night that their car was on fire with their child inside.

"Do we know how the blaze started?" I asked.

Daniels shook his head.

The car still smoldered and hissed after the flames were extinguished.

Brenda and the forensics investigators went to work.

"The blaze started on this side of the vehicle," an arson investigator said as he pointed to the driver's side door. He carefully examined the window frame, along with the A- and B-pillars.

It was an odd place for a vehicle fire to start. Most started in the engine, the electrical system, or the fuel line.

"This is really weird. Look at this blanching here." He pointed toward the exterior door, his face crinkling with confusion. "If I didn't know better, I'd say this fire started outside the car."

"Maybe it did," I said.

"Not really sure what would cause this type of burn pattern, except, maybe, a flamethrower."

He poked his head in and surveyed the interior of the vehicle.

"Maybe that's exactly what caused it," I said.

I spoke with Bo Chandler. He wore a drab green duty shirt, forest green trousers, and a straw duty hat. Bo was a tall guy, 6'2", late 30s.

"You see anything suspicious in the area?"

"Not until I came upon the vehicle."

"What time was that?"

"I'd say half an hour ago." He frowned as he surveyed the charred remains.

"Any security footage in the park?"

"We have a cam on the beach and at the entrance. But that entrance cam only lasts a few days before someone vandalizes it. You're more than welcome to take a look at the footage."

We hopped into his electric cart and cruised to the main office. Bo pulled up the footage on the computer at his desk. There was nothing available from the front gate. The beach cam panned from side to side, streaming live on the internet from the park's website.

The parking lot by the bluff couldn't be seen from the beach cam. The pan of the camera stopped just short. We reviewed the footage from the time of the incident. The amber glow from the flames spilled onto the beach, illuminating the palm trees and sand.

I watched the footage as the blaze continued. A few moments later, a figure stepped into frame. I couldn't believe what I saw.

14

A man in a Santa suit walked away from the blaze like it was no big deal. He had a bag slung over his shoulder, but it didn't look like it contained any presents—a flamethrower perhaps—but no presents. A fake white beard hung from his chin, and curly locks dangled from his red cap. His black belt stretched around his round belly, and his black boots trudged through the soft sand.

I just shook my head. "What happened to spreading joy and goodwill?"

I asked Bo for a copy of the footage. He exported it and emailed it to me. I sent it to Isabella. She could enhance the image and perhaps ID the perp. But there wasn't much to work with. The beard and dark sunglasses obscured Santa's features. I asked her to track cellular data in the area. Maybe the perp was stupid enough to leave his phone on.

We left the office and rejoined the others at the scene.

"We should check all purchases of Santa costumes and check with the agencies for any disgruntled Santas," I said.

"I'll have Denise get on this," Daniels replied.

This time of year, you could rent a Santa for a guest appearance at parties and events. At $150 an hour, it was good money. Of course, the agency took half.

"I'll check with the malls," I added.

Highland Village had a Santa every day during the season for photo ops. They were making a killing. The sitting was free, but they got you on the print sales.

"What the hell makes someone do this?" Daniels muttered.

"You know better than to ask that," I said. "Why is the sky blue? People do messed-up things. Especially around the holidays when they're hurting."

"You think this was targeted or random?" JD asked.

The sheriff shrugged. "That's what you boys are going to find out."

Paris Delaney was a little late to the scene. She hopped out of the van with her crew and got B-roll footage of the smoldering car.

She asked me for a comment. I gave her the basic information and told her that we were looking for a man dressed as Santa. I told her I'd send her a copy of the surveillance footage to broadcast. Perhaps someone would recognize the man, but it was doubtful.

A relationship with the news could be advantageous from time to time.

We wrapped up at the scene and headed back to the marina.

"Just when I think it can't get any more screwed up around here," JD grumbled on the drive.

He dropped me off, and I hustled down the dock to the *Avventura* and finally got to lay my head against the pillow.

The morning wouldn't be pleasant. We had to talk to Milton Bouchard and his wife, Cynthia. I couldn't imagine they'd be in good spirits. It was draining to constantly see so much anguish. It never got any easier. You had to block it out so you could do the job. But it was especially worse when the victims were kids—18 years old. They had their whole lives ahead of them.

Brenda called as I was fixing breakfast in the morning. "We got a positive match for both victims. Dental records confirm Blake Bouchard was behind the wheel. His girlfriend, Clara McCoy, was the passenger. I also found something interesting."

"I'm listening."

"Both victims were shot first, then torched."

"Why bother with the blowtorch?"

"Who knows how these sickos think?" Brenda said. "Maybe he was trying to cover evidence. Make our job harder." She sighed. "I pulled the slugs, and I'm running ballistics. I'll see if there's a match in the database. Arson investigators found propane residue. I guess the flamethrower is one of those models you can get online from the *Ignition Company*."

It was primarily a novelty item that ran on a small propane canister you could get at any hardware store. Legal in all 50 states, except Maryland. It was billed specifically as "Not a flamethrower." The company had sold out 40K units the first day, and now they were trading on the collectors' market for ten times the original purchase price.

"I'll see if we can track down purchase receipts," I said.

"I'll let you know if anything else turns up," Brenda said before ending the call.

I ate breakfast at the dining nook, then called JD. He swung by the marina, and we headed to see Milton Bouchard.

15

The Bouchards lived in a nice house on Mottled Duck Lane. It was on a corner lot and was surrounded by a nice wooden fence topped with horizontal louvers. The pink home had a Spanish-style roof. There was a cobblestone parking area along the shoulder of the road and a pedestrian gate that led into the compound. The garage was on the side of the house on Woodstar Lane.

We parked on the cobblestone, hopped out, pushed through the gate, and strolled to the front door. I rang the bell, and a moment later, Milton answered. He was in his mid 40s with a touch of gray in his brown hair. His hazel eyes were red and puffy, and the bags were accentuated by lack of sleep. He hadn't shaved yet today and looked like he had been through the wringer.

I flashed my badge and made introductions.

He invited us inside and introduced us to his wife. Cynthia had dyed auburn hair that hung just above her shoulders. She had narrow eyebrows, blue eyes, and a wide mouth. She looked equally as haggard, understandably so. She clutched a tissue and blotted her eyes that constantly wept.

Milton offered us a seat in the living room on a cream sofa with a Chesterfield back. The two sat in a loveseat catty-corner, clutching each other's hand for support.

There was a glass coffee table with various knickknacks and a chessboard with neatly arranged figures. It was a nice home.

"I know this is a difficult time, but the sooner we piece this together, the better the odds are of solving the case."

Milton nodded.

"Like I told the sheriff, Blake had my car last night to take out his girlfriend, Clara. I think they were starting to get serious. I just can't imagine who would do something like this."

It was all he could do to hold it together.

"You know if Blake had any enemies? Any recent alter-cations?"

Milton shook his head. "Not that I know of. Blake was an easy-going guy. Everybody got along with him."

Cynthia squeezed his hand. "It's Clara's ex-boyfriend. I warned him about that girl."

"Tell me more about the situation," I said.

"Clara wasn't exactly *available* when they first started dating. She was in a bad relationship when they met. I told him not to fool with her. She was a nice enough girl. But she didn't break up with her boyfriend until after she'd gone on a date with Blake. She obviously didn't know how to end things cleanly. I warned Blake. I told him she would leave him just the same way. Women like that always do."

"What was Clara's ex-boyfriend's name?"

"Reed something. I'm not sure of his last name."

"I take it the two got into an altercation?"

"Reed sent harassing and threatening texts."

"I didn't know that," Milton said.

"That's because you don't pay attention. You don't listen to anything I say. I told you."

"I listen," he defended.

She shook her head with annoyance.

"I'm telling you, Clara jilted Reed, and he took revenge. That's what you need to be looking at."

"We will certainly investigate him," I said.

Her rage gave way to sobs again, and Milton put his arm around her shoulder to comfort her.

We asked them a few more questions, then left them to grieve in peace. We headed across the island to speak with Clara's mother, Sarah.

The two lived in an apartment at *Boardwalk Place.*

It wasn't quite on the boardwalk. It was a few blocks over.

It was a two-story mint green complex with a veranda and a large terrace that circled the units. It had a metal pitched roof and dormer windows. It was a quaint little complex. We parked at the curb, pushed through the gate, and stepped into the lobby. We took the stairs to the second floor and found apartment #203.

Sarah McCoy answered after a few knocks. She was a bottle-blonde in her late 30s with golden hair that spiraled down to her shoulders. She had aqua eyes and coral pink lips. She looked just as distraught as the Bouchards, with red, droopy eyes.

Sarah invited us in and escorted us down the foyer to the living room. "Have a seat. Can I get you a drink?"

"No, thank you."

"You don't mind if I indulge, do you?"

There was a bottle of vodka on the coffee table that she had already dipped into. She filled her glass, took a swig, and leaned back in a chair next to the sofa. "I took the day off work. I just can't believe this has happened."

"We're very sorry for your loss, Mrs. McCoy. What can you tell us about Clara's ex-boyfriend?"

16

"I never liked Reed Masterson," Sarah said with a slight slur. "I kept telling her she could do better. Blake was a nice kid. I could have handled him as a son-in-law. But I figured Clara would get bored and screw that up long before it got that far."

"Did Reed ever get violent with her?" I asked.

"She wouldn't have admitted it if he did. Clara would never want to acknowledge that I was right about him. They sure as hell fought like cats and dogs."

"What about after the breakup?"

"I had to tell him to stop calling here. He got mouthy with me, and I told him that shit wasn't going to fly. I've got a .38 Smith & Wesson. I told him I was more than willing to give him an up-close and personal introduction."

"What about threats?"

"Oh yeah. There were plenty of those. At least until she blocked him on her phone. That's why he started calling me." She paused. "We shared the same cellular plan. You can have access to the records if you'd like."

"That would be helpful."

"You really think he's responsible for this?"

"He's at the top of the list right now."

I gave her my card and thanked her for the information.

We left the apartment and returned to the rental car. I called Denise and asked her to coordinate with Ms. McCoy for Clara's cell records. "What can you tell me about Reed Masterson?"

Her fingers clacked against the keyboard. A moment later, she read from his file. "DUI. Assault and battery. Looks like a bar fight. Other than that, he's clean."

Denise texted me a photo and his physical description. He was 6 feet tall, brown hair, dark eyes, and had a medium build. Reed could have been the Santa in the beach video, except for the belly. But the belly could have been fake as it is with quite a few dress-up Santas.

Reed lived in the *Tilapia Court* apartments on Jaguar Park. I was anxious to hear his side of the story. I had Isabella pull his phone records for good measure.

"This is not a guy I'd want my daughter to date," Isabella said. She read from a list of text messages Reed sent to Clara McCoy's phone. "*I hope you burn in hell. May the fires of damnation consume you. Evil bitch, die, die, die!*' Do I need to go on?"

"That pretty much says it all."

"I don't have any location data for him during the time of the attack. His phone could have been turned off or the battery dead."

"Or he could have shut it off because he knew he was going to do something bad. Can you tell me where he is right now?"

The sound of her fingers dancing across the keyboard filtered through the speaker in my phone. "Right now, it looks like he's at the Bait Shack. At least, that's where you'll find his phone."

I thanked her for the information and ended the call.

JD headed toward Oyster Avenue. We found parking at a meter, and I hopped out and dropped a few quarters in the slot. We strolled the sidewalk to the Bait Shack and pushed inside.

It was a little hole-in-the-wall ice house with weathered siding, a creaky deck, and fake fish on the walls. There were hooks and nets and pictures of local anglers with their catches. Some were impressive. Some, not so much.

We found Reed behind the bar. The flash of my badge seemed to unsettle him. "What can I do for you?"

"What can you tell me about your ex-girlfriend?"

His face crinkled. "Why are you asking about Clara?"

"Because she's dead."

His jaw dropped, and his eyes rounded. "What!?"

"I guess you don't watch the news."

"I'm working all the time. I don't have time to watch much of anything."

There was a flatscreen behind the bar tuned to a 24-hour news station. Though, I'm not sure if the killing had made the national news.

"Were you working last night?"

"Yeah, why?"

"What time?"

"My shift started at 7 PM and ended at 2 AM. I got out of here about 2:45 AM."

"Can anybody verify that?"

"My manager. The waitstaff. Ask around." He flagged down one of the waitresses. "Debbie, where was I last night?"

"Behind the bar," the brunette said.

Debbie wore blue hot pants and a white tank with Bait Shack written across the chest.

"All night?" I asked.

"From what I remember," Debbie said.

She placed an order, and Reed began working on the drinks, scooping ice into glasses. The cubes cracked as he poured liquor over them.

"How did she die?" Reed asked.

"Who died?" the brunette asked, intrigued.

"My ex-girlfriend," Reed said.

The waitress frowned.

"And her new boyfriend," I added.

"That's horrible," the waitress said.

"Somebody took a flamethrower to them at Fort Dawson Park last night."

Both of their eyes rounded in disbelief.

"That was your girlfriend?" Debbie asked Reed.

"Ex-girlfriend," he said.

Quite often, killers will omit the question *how* when you inform them of a friend or loved one's passing. They already know, so it never occurs to them to ask. But as it stood, Reed's whereabouts were accounted for, and he seemed curious, if detached.

"You don't own a flamethrower, do you?" I asked.

Reed's face crinkled. "No. You don't think I was involved, do you?"

"You sent a number of threatening text messages to Clara."

Reed finished mixing drinks and set them on the counter. The cute waitress scooped them up and set them atop her tray. She lingered, waiting to hear the juicy details.

Reed gave her an annoyed glance. "Don't you have customers to attend to?"

She frowned at him, grabbed her tray, and sauntered away.

"I was upset," Reed admitted in a hushed tone. "Maybe I said a few things I shouldn't have."

"I've got a list. You want me to go through them one by one? There are a number of references to fire and damnation."

His face contorted dismissively. "People say all kinds of things when they're hurt and jealous. I loved her."

"You loved her so much that you roasted her alive?"

"What!? You're out of your mind."

I ignored him. "Do you have a Santa suit?"

17

His face crinkled. "No. I don't own a Santa suit. Seriously? Don't you guys have something better to do than harass me?"

"Actually, we do. Don't get any funny ideas about skipping town," I said before we left.

"I didn't do anything," he shouted after us.

JD got a call as we stepped onto the sidewalk. After a brief exchange, he ended the call with a grin on his face. "The moment has come."

I gave him a curious glance.

"Getting rid of the rental. Let's go pick up my new car."

We hopped into the rental and drove to the Porsche dealership. Jack's car was ready for delivery.

Reggie, the sales guy, greeted us with a friendly smile and a firm handshake as we stepped into the showroom. They loved Jack at the dealership. They all saw dollar signs every time he walked through the door.

The showroom was spotless. It smelled like leather, fresh rubber, and oil. The cars were polished to perfection. There was a white GT3 RS with satin black rims, a GT metallic silver Boxster Spyder, and a couple of SUVs. Jack's new 911 Turbo Cabriolet was on display. It was identical to his other car, except for the color. The lava orange paint job was eye-catching. This was not a car that you could ignore when driving down the road. It had the same chalk leather seats, not a bad option for the intense Florida sun.

Reggie gave us a quick tour of the car. "She's a beauty, isn't she?"

JD was like a kid on Christmas morning. His bright eyes soaked in the sleek lines and graceful curves. It had an aggressive stance and was ready to devour the road.

"Take care of this one," Reggie said. "But if you don't, there's more where that came from."

After we marveled at the car for a few moments, Reggie escorted us back to his office, and JD finalized the paperwork. Reggie handed over the keys to Jack's new car, and the deal was done.

JD seemed relieved as he slipped behind the wheel, like putting on a pair of old sneakers or your favorite jeans. We peeled off the protective film on the door sills and other surfaces.

Reggie opened the showroom doors, and JD cranked up the engine. Reggie waved as we rolled the car out.

As soon as we left the lot and turned onto the road, JD stood on the gas pedal. The engine howled, and the acceleration thrust me against the seat. Wind swirled around the cabin, and all was right with the world. After spending a few weeks in a four-cylinder rental car, we'd both forgotten just how fast the Porsche was.

We drove around the island for a while, soaking in the glory of the new vehicle, cruising up and down Ocean Avenue, watching the waves crash against the shore. Tight bikini bottoms jiggled as beauties walked along the sidewalk. It was the middle of winter, but it was summer all year round in Coconut Key. The lava orange definitely drew plenty of stares from pedestrians and motorists alike.

Music blasted through the speakers. I had to turn it down when Daniels called.

"It looks like Paul Brown isn't missing anymore."

18

"Coast Guard pulled a floater out of the water," Daniels said.

Decomposition gases will cause a corpse to float—sometimes even after they'd been weighted down. Quite often, people underestimate just how much weight it takes to keep a body underwater with a belly full of gases.

I frowned. "Have you notified Linda Brown?"

"Not yet.

"And you're sure it's Paul Brown?"

"The ID in his wallet confirms it." Daniels sighed. "You and numb-nuts need to get down here."

"On our way."

I filled Jack in on the situation, and we headed to the Sheriff's Office. We parked in the lot, hustled down the dock, and joined Sheriff Daniels aboard his patrol boat with the medical examiner, and the forensics guys. We cast off the lines and headed out to sea. Daniels throttled up, bringing the patrol boat on plane after we cleared the breakwater.

We raced across the swells, the sun sparkling the sea. Pleasure boats dotted the teal ocean. The engines rumbled, and the wind whipped across the bow. It didn't take long to reach our destination. A couple miles out, we joined the Coast Guard. We pulled alongside their patrol boat and boarded.

Paul's body lay on the deck. The officers didn't want to handle the remains anymore than they had to before Brenda had a chance to take a look. There wouldn't be much evidence to recover, but they wanted to disturb the corpse as little as possible.

A petty officer said, "Helicopter spotted him, and we pulled him aboard."

Paul Brown wore a navy suit, white shirt, and a blue tie with snowflakes and reindeer. The color had drained from his skin. He didn't look too bad, all things considered. I mean, he wasn't going to win a beauty contest. But it could have been worse. His hair was ratty and tousled, and his body bloated. Paul's remains hadn't yet been nibbled on by the creatures of the deep.

Dietrich snapped photos while Brenda pulled on a pair of nitrile gloves and squatted near the remains. She took the body temperature and did a cursory evaluation of the corpse, looking for signs of trauma. It didn't take her long to remark, "Looks like we got something here."

We all waited with bated breath.

"Blunt force trauma to the head," Brenda said. She pointed to the gash in the back of Paul's scalp. "I'm not prepared to say this is a homicide just yet. He could have been hit by a boat in the water. I'll know more when I get back to the lab."

Dieterich snapped more photos.

When Brenda and the forensics guys finished their preliminary evaluation, Paul's body was bagged and transferred aboard the sheriff's patrol boat. The Coast Guard went about their way, and we headed back toward Coconut Key.

"What does your gut tell you?" I asked Brenda.

She shrugged. "At a glance, the object was dull. It didn't have an edge. The skin was split from the pressure of the impact."

"The hull of a boat?"

"Sure. Something dull. Definitely not a crowbar."

We returned to the station, loaded the remains atop a gurney, and I helped Brenda roll it down the dock to her van.

"I'll let you know when I know something," Brenda said.

After Paul's remains were secured inside, I closed the doors to the van, and Brenda slid behind the wheel. She pulled away as Daniels joined me.

Paris and her crew were in the lot, capturing the whole thing on camera.

The sheriff muttered. "You buy into the idea that this guy got drunk and fell overboard?"

"Not really."

"Neither do I. Stay on top of this one. Use those resources of yours."

"You got it."

I called Isabella as Daniels strolled inside. "I need another favor."

"Asking a lot these days, aren't you?"

"It all comes out in the wash."

"I may have some dirty laundry for you to take care of soon."

I knew the information wouldn't be free forever. "What can you dig up on Paul Brown?"

"Probably quite a lot. You know me."

I gave her Paul's information, and she said she'd be in touch.

We walked to the parking lot, where we were accosted by Paris and crew. "Deputy Wild, can you confirm the identity of the remains?"

"Not at this time."

"Is this in any way related to Paul Brown's disappearance?"

"I can't comment at this time."

We hopped into the Porsche, and JD cranked up the engine. Paris wrapped up her segment as we pulled out of the lot and headed to *Diver Down* to get something to eat. She texted me a few moments later. *[I like JD's new car.]*

Teagan greeted us with a cheery smile as we took a seat at the bar. "How's your day going?"

"A dead body and some grieving parents," JD said. "If you don't count that, not too bad." He smiled. "I got my new car."

Teagan's eyes brightened. She looked past him and scanned the lot. She erupted when she saw it. "I knew you were going to get orange. I had a vision."

"You're psychic powers coming back?" I asked.

"No," she snapped adamantly.

Teagan didn't want anything to do with the paranormal. She had the belief that her supposed abilities were nothing but bad news. As she described it, they ebbed and flowed.

"I'll book us a flight to Vegas if you think you're *on* again."

"Absolutely not. And I am not *on* again. Remember what happened last time you took me gambling?"

"If she really had psychic powers, she'd know I'm ready for another beer," Harlan griped.

Teagan rolled her eyes.

She grabbed an ice-cold longneck from the well, snatched the bottle opener from her back pocket, and popped the top with a hiss. She holstered the bottle-opener like a gunslinger and delivered the brew to the old Marine.

"Much obliged," he said with a smile.

Paris Delaney's segment flashed on the screen behind the bar.

Teagan sauntered back toward us. "You guys want lunch?"

"Indeed," JD replied. "I'll take the pulled pork."

"Ham and cheese sandwich," I said.

"Coming right up." Teagan moved to the register and punched in our order.

Brenda called while we waited to be served. "Well, this is interesting."

19

"Paul Brown had water in his lungs," Brenda said. "That means he was alive when he hit the water. But usually, I see more trauma and propeller wounds when a snorkeler or diver is hit by a boat. It's not pretty when that happens." She paused. "This is too clean."

"Like he was struck by an object on purpose?"

"I'd say."

"Like what?"

"Like I said, there was no edge to the instrument. The skull is fractured and caved in. I'll know more soon, but there was likely brain trauma, intracranial hemorrhaging, and swelling."

I thought for a moment. "A wine bottle?"

"Could be. Sure."

"He was at a party after all."

"I'll keep you posted."

I thanked her and ended the call.

Teagan served lunch, and we chowed down. Isabella called back toward the end of the meal. "I have info."

"Do tell."

"Judging by his credit card receipts, Paul Brown spent a lot of time in Forbidden Fruit," Isabella said.

"He was in sales."

"I guess he did a pretty good job because West-Tek just landed a lucrative deal. But that didn't seem to help Paul's situation. Just looking over his accounts, the guy was in a lot of debt. Living well beyond his means."

"A lot of people do."

"And his wife just took out a $2 million insurance policy on him last month."

That piqued my interest. "That's certainly a motive for whacking your husband over the head and pushing him overboard. Especially if he's diddling a coworker."

"Hope that's helpful."

"It is. What was the contract for?"

"Advanced Intelligent Battlefield Combat Information System. A smart scope that tracks motion with threat assessment, identifies targets, and is proven to eliminate friendly fire incidents. The scopes are networked and provide real-time battlefield information to field units and command operations, including 3-D terrain mapping. And get this.

The units come with the Advanced Optic Display System—smart glasses for remote sighting. Comes in handy when shooting around corners. You don't have to poke your head out and get shot anymore."

"Sounds like a hell of a system."

"The Marine Corps seems to think so. They bought $292 million worth of optics and support. If the devices are adopted across all branches, it could be a multibillion-dollar contract."

"Is this public knowledge?"

"The details are vague, but the contract is listed on the DoD website. Buy stock in the company now," she joked.

Maybe it wasn't a joke.

I chuckled and thanked her for the info.

We headed across town to speak with Paul's wife, Linda. I was interested to see what she had to say. She lived in the Fillmore Tower. The couple had a nice condo on the 23rd floor.

We pulled into the lot, and JD drove to the valet stand under the awning. He was a little hesitant handing over the keys to his new ride. JD flashed his badge and instructed the valet to keep it close. He gave him a nice tip to seal the deal.

The kid hopped into the car, moved it a few feet, and kept it upfront by the entrance.

The concierge buzzed us into the lobby. We'd had dealings with him before. He wasn't always as pleasant as the concierge at the Trident. But he forced a smile and tried to be accommodating."Good afternoon, gentlemen. What can I do for you?"

"We're here to see Linda Brown."

"Should I let her know you're here?"

"That won't be necessary," I said.

We made our way to the bank of elevators, and JD pressed the call button. The concierge always liked to give residents a heads up to stay on their good side.

The door slid open, and we stepped aboard. The elevator launched us to the 23rd floor, and we quickly found apartment #2312. I banged on the door, and Linda Brown answered a few moments later. With tissue in hand, she blotted her weepy eyes. "Please come in."

"We're deeply sorry for your loss, Mrs. Brown," I said.

She escorted us down the foyer and into the living room, where she offered us a seat on the sofa. The apartment had a pretty typical layout for the building—floor-to-ceiling windows with a view of the ocean, a nice terrace, an open kitchen, and two bedrooms.

"The sheriff called," she said between sobs. "He said there's a possibility that Paul was murdered."

"We don't have anything conclusive yet. But it looks suspicious. After the incident with Kevin Gardner, are you sure the two remained separated for the rest of the evening?"

"I'm not sure of anything at this point."

"It's possible that your husband was struck with a blunt instrument. Perhaps a wine bottle."

Her face tightened, and her eyes filled.

I casually shifted the conversation. "It's my understanding you recently took out a life insurance policy."

She stopped sniffling and stared at me—concern filling her eyes.

20

L inda swallowed hard. "Yes, I took out an insurance policy. Paul thought it would be best. He'd taken on a lot of debt. He was terrible at investing. He just picked loser after loser. Everybody else's portfolio went to the moon while ours sank. He had no business managing finances, I'll tell you that."

Her eyes flicked between the two of us, waiting for absolution.

"Besides Kevin Gardner, were there other coworkers he had issues with?" I asked.

She hesitated. "I see the way you are looking at me. You don't think I had something to do with Paul's death, do you?"

"It's routine to give a little extra scrutiny to spouses," I said. "After all, you are coming into $2 million."

"That's going to be barely enough to keep me afloat. There's the mortgage on the condo, the boat, the cars... And don't you dare say the word downsize. I like my life just as it is. As it was." Her eyes filled again. "I loved Paul, despite his flaws."

"Like I was saying... any other coworkers Paul might have had issues with?"

She thought for a moment. Then said, tentatively, "Preston Brinkman, maybe."

"What was the issue?"

"I don't know. I think Preston thought he should be in charge of the sales team instead of Paul. He's a dorky little guy with poor social skills and a disagreeable attitude."

"He ever make any threats?"

"Oh, no," she said, dismissing the notion. "Nothing like that. I'm just trying to be thorough."

"Can you account for Preston's whereabouts after Paul and Kevin got into their squabble?"

"I don't remember. Honestly, the whole thing is a blur right now. It doesn't seem real. I can't believe Paul's really dead. I keep thinking he's going to walk through that door." She sobbed again.

I waited for her to pull herself together. I hated to ask the question when she was already so upset. "Do you think Paul was having an affair with Kim Gardner?"

She took a deep breath. "He told me he wasn't, and I have to believe that."

"Any idea why Kevin Gardner was so adamant about it?"

"He's a loser. He sponges off Kim, and he's terrified she's going to leave him. He doesn't have a job. I don't know what she sees in him." She paused and blotted her eyes. "I just don't understand how this happened. I mean..." She stopped and thought for a moment. "I guess I did see Kevin go toward the day head after the fight."

"Do you remember how long he was gone?"

She shrugged.

"That contradicts the statements by other guests."

She scoffed. "How much attention were people paying to him? I mean, do you know when every person on a yacht makes a trip to the head? No. Of course not." She paused. "I'm not saying Kevin killed him, but whoever did was on that boat. And you have a list of every person aboard, don't you?"

I nodded.

"So, they're not going to get away with this."

"We'll do everything we can to apprehend the perpetrator."

I dug my hand into my pocket, pulled out my card, and slid it across the coffee table. "Thank you for your time. Sorry to disturb you. If you can think of anything else, please don't hesitate to call."

"You'll let me know if anything comes up."

I nodded.

We stood up, and she escorted us through the foyer. She closed and latched the door after we were in the hall. As we strolled to the elevator, JD asked, "What do you think?"

I shrugged.

The call button lit up as JD pressed it. The doors slid open. We stepped aboard and plunged down to the lobby. The valet pulled the Porsche around as we stepped outside, and Jack hopped behind the wheel.

We cruised to the West-Tek headquarters on the east side of the island. The main office took up the entire fourth floor of the Empire One building. With floor-to-ceiling windows, the office had a stunning view of the ocean. The interior was decorated in a sleek, minimalist style, reflecting the cutting edge nature of the business.

This wasn't just a cookie-cutter office with boring cubicles and employees imprisoned like inmates. The floor plan was open, and there was an array of workstations with large flatscreen displays. There were standing desks, sitting desks, and treadmill desks. There was a recreational area with bean bag chairs and yoga balls, a set of weights, a stair machine, and a few workout machines.

It also had a full kitchen—not just a microwave. If you wanted to grill a steak, you could. The refrigerator was always stocked with sodas, water, fruit juices, and even beer for those after-hour celebrations. *Sometimes before-hour celebrations.* There was on-site daycare for employees with budding families.

It didn't look like a workspace at all. More of a playspace. Employees had the freedom to do their own thing as long as they got the job done.

A receptionist greeted us at the main desk. After we flashed our badges, she contacted Alexandria and let her know we were here. "She'll be right with you. Just take a seat."

JD and I plopped down on the leather sofa and started perusing through magazines on the coffee table. There was a flatscreen display tuned to a 24-hour news channel, but the volume was muted.

Jenson Ward greeted us with a smile. "Alexandria is on a call right now. She'll be with you shortly. Can I get you anything? Water, coffee, beer?"

JD was about to take him up on a beer.

"No, thank you," I said.

Jack frowned.

"I heard they found Paul. Leaves me with a heavy heart." Jenson shook his head. "Making any headway?"

"Here and there."

"Well, if there's anything I can do, let me know. I liked Paul. He could rub some people the wrong way, but we got along."

"Who did he rub the wrong way?"

Jenson shrugged. "His wife, for one." He chuckled. "I mean, we all irritate our wives, don't we? We're lucky they put up with us."

"Some of them don't," JD said.

Jenson smiled.

"How long have you been married?" I asked.

"Five years of bliss," he said in a dry tone. "And two wonderful kids. Gabby and Gavin."

He pulled out his phone and displayed a few pics with pride.

"You have a beautiful family," I said.

"Thank you."

"Getting back to the Christmas party," I said, "when was the last time you saw Paul?"

"Like I told you before, I helped the Colonel and Tom break things up. I had a few words with Paul, trying to calm him down. Then he went to the day head. I never saw him after that."

"And you stayed in the salon?"

"Yes. I tried to smooth things over and assure our high-profile guests that this was not the way we handled business in the company."

I'd asked all these questions before at the party. But it's always good to see if someone's story changes over time.

"What about Kevin Gardner? I'm getting conflicting stories. Was he ever out of your view after the fight?"

Jenson thought for a moment, then shrugged. "I don't know. I can't be sure. It was a hectic time. You don't think Kevin helped Paul overboard, do you?"

"Anything is possible."

"I guess," he replied, not sure what to make of it all. "I mean, things were pretty heated between them."

I gave him my card and told him to call me if he could remember any other details that might be helpful.

Jenson excused himself, and a few minutes later, Alexandria greeted us in the lobby. She looked as stunning as ever, this time in a Navy blue off-the-shoulder dress that hugged her svelte form.

We stood up to greet her and shook hands.

She frowned. "I heard the horrible news. I've assured Linda that we will help her during this difficult transition. The company will be covering all burial expenses."

"That's kind of you," I said.

"As I mentioned, Paul was a valued employee. I spoke briefly with Jenson just now. It seems you think Paul may have been murdered. Do you have any leads?"

"We're not ruling out anything at this point."

She gave us a brief tour before ushering us into her private office to speak. She closed the glass door and offered us a seat in two chairs across from her desk. Alexandria took a seat behind her desk and sat tall in a power-pose. "So, how can I be of assistance? I've already told you everything I know."

"I just have a few follow-up questions. And I need to speak with one of your employees."

"To be honest, I'm a little shocked. I've vetted all my employees thoroughly. Extensive background and personality checks. It's disturbing to me that I hired someone who may be capable of such a heinous act. It's hard to wrap my head around." She took a deep breath, then blew it out. "I guess your next question is going to be who do I think is capable of such a thing?"

"You're very perceptive," I said.

"My job is all about anticipation. It's crucial for me to be able to read a room, know what kinds of questions people will ask before they ask them, and provide solutions for problems they don't know they have."

"From what I understand, you're providing a very lucrative solution to the Marine Corps."

"You seem to stay on top of government contracts, Deputy."

"I have sources."

She regarded me with curiosity.

"What about Preston Brinkman?"

Alexandria pondered the question, then looked through the glass wall of her office and surveyed the employees at their workstations. "I'm not suggesting anything, mind you, but Preston *was* passed over for promotion. It's safe to say there was a little animosity toward Paul after that. Though I seriously doubt he's capable of murder. I guess you never know what someone is capable of until they get into a situation."

"True."

"But, Preston?" Her face crinkled, and she shook her head. "No way."

"Are you sure that Kevin Gardner wasn't anywhere near Paul after the incident between them?"

"I can't be sure. I was darting about, mingling with the guests, trying to maintain some sort of order amid the chaos. It's what I do. Damage control. Putting out fires.

Being a CEO is all about solving other people's problems in an efficient manner."

"That's what your CFO said."

"Jenson takes a lot of my overflow."

"And the last time you saw Paul Brown?"

"As I mentioned. In the companionway near the day head."

"And did you have words at that time?"

"Don't quote me on this, but I recall saying something about keeping his personal business out of office affairs."

"Did you know about the affair with Kim Gardner?"

"Has that been confirmed? Is there concrete proof?"

"Kevin Gardner seems to think it was confirmed."

"It's against company policy. But honestly, if someone's getting their job done, meeting their quotas, and bringing in revenue, I don't really care what they do on their personal time."

"Paul was good at his job?"

"Very. He'd developed an impressive list of inside contacts, and he could sell ice to Eskimos."

"I'm sure he was paid handsomely in reward."

"With commissions and bonuses, Paul was going to draw damn near as much money as I do. Although, admittedly, I take a modest salary and pump it all back into the business."

"Seems like business is good."

She smiled. "There's always a war somewhere."

That hung there for a moment.

"I know it's terrible to say. But wars will go on long after you and I have left the planet. If I can make the battlefield safer for our boys, then I figure I'm doing a good thing. Nothing wrong with making a buck or two in the process. At least, that's how I live with myself."

I lifted an intrigued brow. Alexandria West was a piece of work, and she knew it.

"I know, I know. I must sound cold and heartless to you. The world is a cold place, as I'm sure you know."

"It can be warm and cozy at times," I said, playing devil's advocate.

"I'm all about warm and cozy. But you can kiss warm and cozy goodbye without superior firepower. Because somebody will come and take it away from you. When somebody kicks down your front door and storms your property with automatic rifles, threatening your family, what do you want on your side? A book on psychology so you can try to talk them down? Or a high-powered assault rifle with extra magazines?"

The woman had a point.

"What about you? Did you have any animosity toward Paul?"

21

"So, I'm a suspect now?" Alexandria paused. "Of course I am. Everybody that was on the boat is. Look, I liked Paul. He was my top salesman. He brought in a lot of business and closed a lot of deals."

"A real rainmaker," I said.

"You bet. And I don't know if he can be replaced."

"Don't your products sell themselves?"

"Our latest one does," she said, her face beaming with pride. "But you know how this business is. It takes contacts, relationships, wining and dining, a great product, and the right deal. You can build a better mousetrap, but if the world doesn't know it exists, it's not going to sell. And sometimes you have to educate the customer on why they need your product."

There was a long silence as we stared at each other.

"Look, gentlemen. I want to help you as best I can. I'm deeply troubled by the idea that Paul was murdered. I'm all about efficiency, and my time is precious. I don't want to waste any more of my time or yours chasing down bogus leads. If you think I had something to do with Paul's disappearance, I'm happy to take a lie detector test."

"As you're aware, those aren't admissible in court."

"I'm not talking about a court of law. I'm talking about you and me. Will that satisfy your curiosity so you can go about the business of solving this thing?"

"If you're willing and want to come down to the station. I have no problem with that."

"No need to go to the station." She held up her phone. "I have an app on my phone that we've designed specifically for interrogations. It's a voice stress analyzer. In our evaluations, it has been as effective, or more so, than a traditional polygraph."

"You expect me to trust an app you developed?"

Her face crinkled, not sure how to respond. "Should I be insulted by that statement?"

I chuckled. "I'm sure it functions properly. But as its creator, I'm sure you know how to beat it."

She looked at me flatly. "I didn't program the damn thing. I hired somebody to do it. I'm an idea person. I leave the coding and development to other people. I'm not the cook. I just get people into the restaurant." She paused. "We can try it on you if you would like to see its accuracy?"

The concept amused me, and I wanted to see the app.

She launched the app on her phone and followed through the prompts that guided the operator. "I need to ask a series of control questions."

I knew how the drill worked. All lie detectors worked basically the same. They needed to calibrate a baseline of truthful answers, then measure against irregularities in pulse, respiration, and blood pressure. Some people were good at beating the tests. They'd elevate their vitals during the control questions. Some people went as far as putting tacks in their shoes to inflict pain, creating an involuntary reaction. But that trick was pretty well known by most operators.

Without electrodes hooked to my body, a blood pressure cuff, and a heart monitor, I wasn't sure how accurate this thing could be.

Alexandria attached a small device to the port on her phone. It was an infrared camera. She aimed the lens at me as she began asking control questions. "The camera measures heat fluctuations in your face as well as pupillary response. It can detect pulse rate more accurately than any on body monitor." She paused. "Are you ready?"

I nodded.

"What's your name?"

"Tyson Wild."

"What city are we in?"

"Coconut Key."

"Is it raining?"

"No."

"Are you single?" she asked in a flirty tone.

"Yes."

"Do you find me attractive?"

"I've seen worse."

She frowned at me playfully. "*Yes* or *no* answers, please."

"Yes."

She smiled, and her blue eyes sparkled. "Okay. Let's get to the fun stuff."

"I'm an open book," I said, which wasn't exactly the truth.

"Have you ever done anything illegal?"

"No."

She arched a curious eyebrow. "Are you sure?"

"Yes."

"Do you like working as a deputy?"

"Yes."

"Have you ever killed anyone before?"

"No," I said in the same even tone as all my answers.

"Have you served in the military?"

"Yes."

"Have you ever been involved in any clandestine operations?"

"No."

JD seemed amused by the process and my answers.

"Have you ever stolen a car?"

"No."

"Have you lied to spare someone's feelings?"

"No," I lied.

"What color are my eyes?"

"Brown." Now she knew I was lying.

Her eyes watched the screen—her face crinkled with frustration, not getting the answers she wanted.

"Have you ever done anything you regret?"

"No," I lied again. "This is starting to sound like a therapy session."

"Getting to the truth can be painful."

"I don't know if we're getting to the truth. I'm not sure that little app of yours works."

Her brow knitted, perplexed. "I don't understand. I know you lied on some of the answers, but it's telling me no deception detected."

"Maybe you need to have a talk with the guys who programmed the app," I teased.

She scowled at me lightheartedly. "How did you do that?"

"Machines can be beaten."

"I'm still willing to take a poly."

"Come down to the station."

"I'll clear out my schedule." She smiled. "Is there anything else you would like to ask me?"

I glanced at JD, and I could see lewd thoughts brewing behind his eyes.

"Not at the moment," I said, "But I would like to talk to Preston before we leave."

"Certainly." She hesitated. "Can you do me a favor? Can you work with my app developer to troubleshoot the analyzer? I want to know how you beat it. That's never happened before."

"Maybe you haven't been testing your product on the right people."

"Maybe not," she said, staring at me with intrigued eyes. "Want a job as a product tester?"

"I have a job."

"This one pays well."

"I don't need the money." I smiled.

"A man that can't be bought. I like that."

She stood up and walked around the desk, pushed open her office door, and called to Preston, "The deputies would like to speak with you for a moment?"

He gave a hesitant glance, then his nervous eyes flicked to us. Preston left his workstation and walked toward the office.

"I'll leave the office to you," Alexandria said to me.

She stepped aside and let Preston enter. Sweat was already misting his forehead.

22

Preston was a nerdy guy with bushy brown hair, a narrow face, a big nose, and thick glasses. His brown eyes looked like they were squinting all the time. He wore a classic gray herringbone plaid three-piece suit with a maroon bow tie.

At first glance, this guy couldn't kill anyone. But as I thought about it, he was that quiet coworker that holds it all inside, finally snaps, and takes the whole office out.

"Have a seat," I said, motioning to Alexandria's empty chair.

He shook his head. "Oh, no. That's Ms. West's chair. Nobody sits in Ms. West's chair."

I stood up and offered him mine. He obliged, and I sat against the edge of the desk.

His nervous eyes flicked between the two of us.

"I just want to warn you, I don't do well in high-pressure situations."

"This isn't high-pressure," I said.

"Yeah, it is. Interviews with cops. Even cops like you two... My stomach's already getting upset."

"Don't worry. It's just a few simple questions."

He nodded.

"Did you see the altercation between Kevin Gardner and Paul Brown?"

He nodded.   .

"Where were you at the time?"

"In the salon, as I recall."

"And what did you do after they were separated?"

"I had another drink and tried to make conversation. I'm not very good at conversation."

"But these are your coworkers. You must have something to talk about in a social setting?"

He shook his head. "I really don't have much interaction with people. I show up, I do my thing, I go home."

"But you're in sales. How does that work exactly if you're not comfortable in social situations?"

"Well, I'm really good with the technical side of things. I have a photographic memory. I can recall a lot of details. It comes in handy when listing off specs for devices. Nobody else can do what I do." He pointed to the staff. "All these people need me. And they know it. I'm the one they call when they need someone to close the sale with technical information. Every single one of them brings me along to seal the deal. They don't know how this stuff works. None of them. They all sell the sizzle, but I sell the steak."

"I see. What can you tell me about the Advanced Intelligent Battlefield Combat Information system?"

He hesitated, and his eyes flicked between the two of us again. "I can't discuss it unless you have the proper clearance."

"I hear you were upset about Paul leading the sales team."

His jaw tensed, and the veins in his temples pulsed. "I know all the systems inside and out. Better than anyone else. I should be leading the sales team. Instead, they bring me out like some kind of circus monkey to do tricks to impress the clients with technical know-how."

"Sounds like you're pretty mad about it?"

"It's not fair."

"Mad enough to whack a coworker over the head with a wine bottle?"

His face twisted. "What are you talking about?"

I shrugged. "I don't know. Maybe you were so upset that Paul was leading the sales team instead of you that you decided to do away with him."

"So, I'm a suspect now?"

"We're just asking a few friendly questions."

"There's nothing friendly about these questions. And I am under no obligation to speak with you any further." He

stood up and straightened his suit. "Good day, gentlemen."
He pushed out of the office and walked back to his station.

Alexandria reentered her office. "I hope he was cooperative?"

"To a degree, until it got sticky. Do you recall where he was
after the fight?"

Alexandria thought for a moment as she stood by the door.
Her pretty blue eyes gazed out across the office, watching a
frazzled Preston at his computer. "I'm pretty sure he was on
the aft deck."

"I don't see that guy dragging Paul's body around and
hoisting it over the gunwale without anybody seeing it," JD
said. "A strong wind would knock him over."

Jack had a point.

"How long will a poly at the station take?" Alexandria asked.

I shrugged. "Sometimes as little as 30 minutes. Sometimes 2
hours or more."

"I've got nothing to hide, so let's get this out of the way. I'll
wrap up some things here and meet you at the station in
half an hour."

"Sounds good to me."

We had a few conversations with random employees on the
way out. A few of them confirmed that Preston had been
milling about the salon in the aft deck after the altercation
between Paul and Kevin.

At the station, the tech prepared the polygraph.

Daniels found us. "I know you've got a lot on your plate right now, but I need you guys to look into this Christmas light thing."

"We've been looking into it."

"No, I mean the new developments."

"There are new developments?"

"It's escalated just a tad."

23

"The judges for *Lights in the Heights* just received death threats," Daniels said. "All three of them. Judy Leigh, Janet Cook, and Herman Moore. Get over to Whispering Heights after you finish here and see if there's any merit to this."

"You got it," I said.

Daniels gave me the addresses and contact info for the judges.

Alexandria arrived, and she was hooked up to the electrodermal sensors that measured sweat gland activity, upper and lower respiratory monitors that wrapped around her chest, a blood pressure cuff, and a pulse monitor. Polygraphs were all about fear and intimidation. They were an interrogation tool, mainly used to elicit confessions. There was nothing scientifically conclusive about the results. A polygraph measures nervousness. And a lot of suspects crack under the perceived pressure. Alexandria's app would never be as intimidating as this device in this type of setting.

I sat in the conference room with the tech and JD. I asked a series of control questions interspersed with relevant questions. Alexandria smiled and didn't seem the least bit flustered.

"Are you the CEO of West-Tek?"

"Yes."

"Were you present the night of Paul Brown's disappearance?"

"Yes."

"Have you ever committed a crime?"

"Of course."

I lifted a curious eyebrow.

"We all break laws. I can't drive the speed limit." She smiled.

"Have you ever committed a felony?"

"No."

"Were you involved in Paul Brown's death?"

I watched the computer screen as it displayed her vitals.

"No."

The waves on the screen were as flat as a lake on a day with no wind.

"Do you know who murdered Paul Brown?"

"No."

There was still no reaction.

I asked the same question in a number of different ways, interspersed with more control questions. Her reaction was always the same and did not indicate deception.

I stared at the computer screen and pretended to grow concerned. I exchanged a worried glance with the tech, then my eyes flicked back to Alexandria. "You sure you had no involvement in the death of Paul Brown or the disposal of his remains?"

"How many different ways are you going to ask me that?"

"Just answer the question."

"No."

The display was even, but I lied. "The unit indicates deception."

She laughed. "Well, your unit is broken."

I stared at her for a long moment. "We know you killed Paul Brown."

"You can't be serious?"

"The machine indicates deception," I said innocently.

Her eyes narrowed at me. "Show me."

I exchanged another glance with the tech, then looked back at Alexandria. "I'm sorry, that's against protocol."

She laughed. "I bet you're a good poker player, Deputy. But I just called your bluff. You know, and I know, that I've answered these questions truthfully. The machine didn't pick up any deception. Nice try."

She proceeded to disconnect the monitoring devices.

"If you'll excuse me, gentlemen. I have a company to run." She stood up and pushed away from the table.

"We appreciate your cooperation." I stood up and we shook hands. "Thanks for coming in."

She smirked and strolled out of the conference room. I followed her into the hall.

"Tell me, Deputy. Does that tactic often work?"

"You'd be surprised."

"You know where to find me if you need me," she said as she sauntered down the hallway, her high heels clacking against the tile.

JD muttered in my ear, "What do you think?"

"I think she's telling the truth, or she's a complete sociopath."

"Well, you're attracted to her. She must be crazy," JD quipped.

I gave him a look. He had no room to talk.

We left the station, hopped into the Porsche, and zipped to *Whispering Heights.* Judy Leigh lived a block over from Esther Murray in a lemongrass green bungalow with a white scalloped picket fence and a nice veranda. A Plasma Yellow Pearl Subaru Crosstrek Premium was parked at the curb.

"Who is it?" Judy asked through the door after we knocked.

"Coconut County, ma'am. We're responding to the death threat you received."

"How do I know you two are cops?"

I held my badge to the peephole.

"That could be fake."

"It's not fake, ma'am."

"You don't look like cops. You look like vagrants."

I chuckled. "I don't look like a vagrant."

"Your friend does."

I laughed again, and Jack's face twisted into a scowl.

"Ma'am, look at the curb," JD said, pointing to his Porsche. "Do vagrants drive cars like that?"

"You could have stolen it."

"Call the sheriff and ask him to give you a description of the two deputies he sent to talk to you about the death threat."

She was silent for a few moments, then pulled open the door after she had called the department.

Judy was a petite woman a little past 60. Maybe a lot past 60. She had silver hair that was teased with way too much hairspray and seemed to spiral in all directions. She wasn't light-handed with the eyeliner or the makeup either. The heavy base made her skin look even, but it stopped at her jawline, making her wrinkled neck and chest stand out, red and spotted from the sun.

"I'm sorry for the trouble. But you just can't be too careful these days, especially with what's been happening recently. And with the letter I received..."

"Do you still have the letter?" I asked.

"Of course. It's evidence. I put it in a Ziploc bag. Let me get it for you."

She spun around and darted down the foyer into the house. She returned a moment later with the letter in a large Ziploc. I snapped on a pair of nitrile gloves for good measure, and she handed it to me.

"Has anyone else touched this?" I asked.

"Just me."

"How did you receive it?"

"It came in the mail."

"You have the envelope?"

"Oh dear, I think I might have thrown it away." Her face tensed with worry. "I'll go check."

She spun around and waddled down the foyer, disappearing again into the living room.

I took the opportunity to examine the threat. It was printed on regular paper by an inkjet printer. I could see the print banding and the misalignment of the printhead. The font was an oversized varsity-style lettering. Something you'd see on a sports jersey or cheerleader's uniform.

The note read: *If Esther Murray wins again, you all die.*

Direct and to the point. It was signed: *Merry Christmas. Ho, ho, ho!*

Judy returned a moment later with the envelope clasped between a pair of tongs.

I asked her for another Ziploc so as not to cross-contaminate the evidence. Once again, she disappeared into the house and returned a moment later. I bagged the evidence and examined the envelope. It was a standard *peel and stick* forever stamp. The letter had been mailed yesterday. It had a Coconut Key ZIP code. With a little digging, we might be able to find out where exactly it was mailed from. The envelope was addressed to Judy and printed with an inkjet as well. There was no handwriting or return address anywhere on the envelope or the letter.

"You have any idea who's behind this?" Judy asked.

"The forensics lab will take a look. They may be able to determine the model of printer used. It's possible we could track the sales of those units and narrow it down."

"It's amazing what you can do these days, isn't it?" she said.

I agreed.

"How much danger do you think I'm really in?"

"That's hard to say. Do you live alone, ma'am?"

She nodded. "My husband passed away a few years ago."

"I'm sorry for your loss."

"I'm not. He was a pain in the ass." She confided in a whisper. "God rest his soul. To be honest, I'm having the time of my life. I do wine Wednesdays with the girls. And when I'm feeling lonely, I get on Silver Seductions and satisfy my urges," she said with a naughty smile.

"Good for you."

"I guess you could call me a little bit of a cougar." She batted her false lashes at me, and her blue eyes sparkled.

"I heard you're looking into Carol Anderson for the destruction of Esther's lighting arrangement."

"We don't discuss ongoing cases."

"You think she's responsible for the letter?" Judy asked in a whisper.

"We'll see what the lab says."

"I wouldn't put it past her. She's desperate to win."

"I hope this letter won't affect your judging," I said.

She puffed up, standing tall. "I will not be intimidated."

"Good for you," I said.

"I'll have the sheriff double the patrols in the neighborhood. Don't open your door for strangers. And maintain good situational awareness."

"I will. And I've got old Betsy in case the shit hits the fan."

"Old Betsy?"

"My Glock 9mm."

"Sounds like you're going to be just fine."

I thanked her. As we were leaving, she said, "Feel free to stop by anytime, Deputy. I'll let you know if any more threats turn up."

"Thank you."

She watched from the doorway as we strolled the walkway, past the gate, and climbed into the Porsche. Jack cranked up the engine and muttered. "She's a cougar, alright. She belongs in the zoo."

I stifled a chuckle.

"Be nice."

"I thought she was going to pounce on you for a second."

I smiled and waved at Mrs. Leigh as JD pulled away from the curb.

"I think she's more your type."

Jack scowled at me.

We talked to the two other judges, and they both had the same story. We collected their letters as evidence, tried to soothe their nerves, and assuage their fears.

We returned to the station, logged the letters, and filled out reports.

Denise poked her head into the conference room with a strange look on her face. "There's a guy on the phone asking for you."

"Me?" I replied. "What does he want?"

She frowned. "He won't say. Says he'll only talk to you."

JD and I exchanged a curious glance.

"What about me?" JD asked, feeling left out.

"He didn't say anything about you."

That twisted Jack's face into a frown.

24

"T his is Deputy Wild."

"I killed them," the caller said.

"You killed who?"

"Whom. You killed whom?"

"Grammar aside, who did you kill?"

"Who do you think?"

"I'm not psychic," I said. "If you haven't noticed, a lot of people get murdered around here. Care to be more specific?"

We got a lot of crackpots calling the department, so I wasn't taking it too seriously.

"The couple by the beach."

"That was you?"

"That's what I just said."

I had taken the call at Denise's desk. She stood by with JD, listening. I put it on speaker so they could hear and mouthed the words, track the call. "Why did you kill the couple?"

"They deserved it."

"They were just kids."

"They were far from innocent."

"Is that how you're justifying it?"

"I'm not justifying anything. I know what I did was wrong. But that's not going to stop me from doing it again."

"Why?"

"Why not?"

"I can think of quite a few reasons why not. One, it's illegal. Two, you're causing a great deal of suffering. Three, you're throwing your life away."

"My life is shit. You don't know anything about my life."

"Tell me more."

He laughed. "I'm not going to tell you anything that will help you catch me."

"You seem pretty confident that you're not going to get caught. Otherwise, you wouldn't have called the station."

"You won't catch me," he said, not a trace of doubt in his voice.

"I wouldn't be so sure about that. I have been known to apprehend a suspect or two in my day."

"I know. I see you quite often on the television with that perky reporter. She's cute."

"She has her qualities."

"She can be annoying at times."

I stifled a chuckle. "I think she sees that as an attribute. How do I know you're really the one responsible?"

"You want details? I can give you details." He paused. "I shot them both with a 9mm. The boy in the chest. The girl in the chest and head. You didn't find any shell casings in the area. I picked those up. Then I torched the car."

"You used a flamethrower from the Ignition Company."

He hesitated for a moment.

"Didn't think I knew that, did you?"

"I expected you would figure it out. There aren't many commercially available options."

"You know I'm going through the list of purchases."

"Good luck. There were 40,000 sold. And how do you know I didn't buy it secondhand? I'm not stupid enough to kill people with anything that can be tracked to a credit card."

"You know I'm tracing this phone call."

"Good luck. This is a burner phone making a VoIP call over an encrypted network routed through multiple proxy servers. In five lifetimes, you wouldn't be able to track this call."

"Seems like you know a thing or two about the tech industry," I said, fishing for any information that might be helpful.

"I know a thing or two about a lot of things." His monotone voice droned on, devoid of any emotion or fear. It was the voice of a man that was burned out on the world and no longer cared about anything, including himself.

"I suppose you see yourself as some type of angel of death."

"I don't believe in angels or devils, Deputy. There is no heaven or hell. Unless you want to call this existence hell. There's only the here and now."

Having technically died once and been given a second chance, I knew a thing or two about the other side. I couldn't say exactly what was beyond the final curtain, but there was something there. I was of the mind that what we did in this life mattered in the next, to some degree or another.

"That's a pretty nihilistic viewpoint," I said.

"It is what it is."

"How would you feel if someone shot you and turned you extra crispy with a flamethrower?"

He paused for a moment. "I suppose I wouldn't like it. But I might be grateful. It would be an end to the incessant pain of living."

"You know there's a simple solution for that. If it's so bad, you could always…"

"Take my own life? Are you encouraging me to commit suicide, Deputy?"

"I'm not encouraging you to do anything. I will, however, encourage you to come down to the station and continue this chat in person."

He laughed. "Sorry. That's not how the game works."

"So this is a game?"

"It's all a game, isn't it? We play games all our lives. We jump through hoops, pursue relationships, chase money, and in the end, we all end up in the same place. The long dirt nap. Nothing that we do here matters. All the knowledge that we gain is lost. All of our relationships fade."

"That's not exactly true. We live on through our children."

"So they can repeat the cycle endlessly. And for what? Someday the Universe will cease to exist, and human beings will vanish. No one gets out alive. What does it matter if I speed up someone's departure?"

"You must be a lot of fun at cocktail parties," I joked.

"I have no need for cocktail parties. I don't like to socialize. I find most of my fellow human beings miserable. Insufferable. No integrity. No spine."

"But you have all of those wonderful qualities?"

"I never said I was perfect."

"That would be a stretch."

"I do what I say I'm going to do. And I'm telling you, I will kill again."

"I have no reason to doubt you," I said. "Perhaps you want to tell me who you're targeting next?"

"Like I said, Deputy. I'm not stupid."

"But this is a game. And if you're confident you won't get caught, why not make it more challenging for yourself?"

He thought for a moment. "I'll take that under advisement."

"What should I call you?"

"The news is calling me the Santa Slayer. I kind of like that, don't you? I'm prone to names with alliteration."

"Have you always lived in Coconut Key?"

"Nice try, Deputy. I'm not giving you any personal information. I think this conversation has gone on long enough. I'll be in touch again soon. I quite enjoyed talking to you. There are not many people I can share this with."

"Well, I'm glad that you called. Must be lonely out there. Have you considered seeing a therapist?"

"Clowns. I'm not going to pay someone $350 an hour to psychoanalyze me and tell me that I need multiple sessions so they can continue to bill insurance. Some joker who went to a liberal arts college who probably doesn't share the same worldview as me is going to advise me on how to live my life?" He scoffed.

"Newsflash. I don't think there are a lot of people that share your particular worldview."

"I think you're mistaken, Deputy. There are a lot of people out there like me. They realize it's a con."

"Life is a con?"

"Wake up, Deputy."

"There's certainly not a lot of people out there torching teenagers just for fun."

"Well, maybe those kids shouldn't have been in the park after dark. You know what they say—nothing good happens after midnight."

He ended the call.

Denise's pretty lips tightened, and she shook her head. "He wasn't lying. The call is untraceable."

25

"This is just great," Daniels grumbled behind his desk as we updated him. "I've got some sicko determined to torch more people, a guy gets bashed in the head at a Christmas party, and death threats over Holiday lights. *Holiday lights!* Is it just me, or do people get a little crazier each year?"

"I don't think it's just you," Denise said.

"Well, then. Why the hell are you standing around? Go solve these things!"

"We're on it," I said.

We left the sheriff's office and made our way back to Denise's desk.

"I called all the Santa temp agencies," Denise said. "They all do extensive background checks on their Santas. Since they are often around children, they can't have any felonies on their record, and certainly no sexual offenses. I've got a call into the charity groups that send Santas to storefronts. And I'm tracking down purchases of Santa suits, but it's just a nightmare. They can be purchased online or in costume shops. I think that's a lost cause, but I'll keep trying.

"Something tells me we don't have a lot of time," I said. "This guy's going to strike again soon."

Denise frowned. "And that sicko was right. It's going to be impossible to track down the purchase of that flamethrower."

"See what you can do."

"He attacked a couple at a known make-out location," Denise said. "He admitted he's planning to do it again. Maybe we should keep a close eye on Fort Dawson."

"He won't strike in the same place," I said. "Unless he's incredibly stupid."

"He didn't sound stupid to me. There's a pattern here."

"One crime does not a pattern make," JD said.

She gave him a friendly scowl. "I'm aware, but I'm saying we will see a pattern emerge over time. We just need to figure out what that pattern is. He's going after couples. Maybe he got burned by a relationship recently, and he's acting out, going after women who look like his ex."

"So he's burning them back," I said.

Denise smiled. "Exactly. Maybe he's targeting those women consciously, or maybe it's subconscious."

"Look at the behavioral psychologist," I teased.

"I've been reading up on the subject matter. There are some really fascinating books out there."

"I know."

"He's going to go after someone with a similar appearance. We should double up on patrols at known make out spots. Secluded places where couples go.'"

"In your *expert* behavioral sciences opinion, can you describe this guy?"

Denise thought about it for a moment. "Statistically speaking, he's a white male in his mid 30s. Lives alone, or maybe with his mother. He's smart and well-spoken, but has social anxiety issues. He has difficulty meeting women. That's why his recent breakup was all the more devastating to him." She grew more and more excited with each revelation as it came to her. "He feels he will never find love again. He typically goes a long time in between relationships because they are so difficult for him to manifest."

"Can you tell me what he ate for breakfast?" JD snarked.

Her pretty emerald eyes narrowed at him. "Mock me all you want. I'll bet my description is pretty close."

"All of this from a few books, huh?"

She smiled with pride. "I'm more than just a desk jockey. And if somebody around here would give me a chance, I could do some real work."

"You do real work," I said. "We couldn't solve these crimes without you."

She smiled again. "I know. But I want to be out there on the street, in the thick of it."

"Come talk to me after you've been shot at a few times."

"I've been in pretty harrowing situations, and I haven't lost my enthusiasm."

That much was true. She'd been in some pretty sticky spots —ones I was worried she might not get out of.

"You know, I don't have any say about what goes on around here. Talk to Daniels," I said. "You don't really want to sweat in a patrol car on a beat all day, do you?"

"I want to get out of the uniform and do plain-clothes stuff."

"I'll help you get out of the uniform," JD joked.

Her eyes narrowed at him. "Keep dreaming." She looked at me. "You know I'm a valuable undercover asset."

"I know. I told the sheriff before, you're an invaluable asset. And I will tell him again."

She gave me a skeptical glance.

I raised my hands innocently.

I couldn't live with myself if anything happened to her.

"You guys get to have all the fun," she said.

JD smiled. "Somebody's gotta do it."

She stuck her tongue out at him. "Go. You've got crimes to solve. And I've got leads to track down."

I smiled at her before leaving.

JD and I strolled through the department, heading toward the main entrance. He looked at his watch. "You know, it's just about happy hour. I think we can kill two birds with one stone."

Mischief brewed in his eyes.

26

Ｗe drove to Oyster Avenue, found a place to park, and strolled the sidewalk. Tourists drifted about, hopping from bar to bar, taking advantage of the specials. The strip was gearing up for the evening. A thin guy in a Santa costume stood on the street corner ringing a bell, taking donations. This time of year, you could find these Santas on sidewalks and at the entrances to drug stores collecting money, canned goods, toys, etc., for the needy.

I surveyed this charity Santa carefully. His build and appearance were completely different from that of our killer. I couldn't help but wonder if we would walk right past our sadistic Santa at some point and not know it.

We made our way to *Forbidden Fruit.* Pumping pop music filtered out of the establishment with booming bass. I gave a nod to the cashier as we stepped into the dim club, and she motioned us inside without a second thought. *This wasn't our first visit.* We stepped inside the club, and the spotlights slashed the hazy air. Girls pranced around the stage in tall stilettos, peeling away bits of skimpy fabric inch by inch, taunting the audience with their supple endowments.

Jacko, the manager, leaned against the bar. His eyes lit up, and he smiled when he saw us. He waved us over, and we greeted each other with a firm handshake. "Gentlemen, what can I do for you today? Business or pleasure?"

In his silver sharkskin suit with a black dress shirt, gold chain, and slicked-back hair, he looked every bit a strip club manager. His eyes surveyed my phone as I displayed a picture of Paul Brown.

"You recognize this guy?" I asked.

He studied the image carefully. "Yeah. In here quite a bit. Good customer. What did he do?"

"He got himself killed."

Jacko's brow lifted with surprise. "No shit?" He frowned and shook his head. "That's a damn shame. Spent a lot of money. The girls loved him. Always brought clients in. Jade's going to be upset."

"Who's Jade?"

"That was his girl. He wasn't shy about spending money with her. Always bringing her gifts."

"What did he get in return?"

Jacko shrugged innocently. "You'll have to ask her about that. I run a clean establishment."

Forbidden Fruit was the premier strip club on the island. But, like all establishments of its kind, there were side negotiations between girls and clients. In a free market, everything can be had for a price.

"Is Jade working today?"

"Yeah." Jacko surveyed the club. His eyes squinted as he peered through the soupy air. He pointed to a luscious brunette with porcelain skin giving a client a pulse-pounding lap dance in the corner of the club by the far wall.

"What you boys drinking?"

"Whiskey," JD said, never one to pass up a free drink.

"First round is on the house," Jacko said.

We weaved through the tables and chairs and took a seat not far from Jade. When the song was over, she collected her tip, put her bra back on, and sat in her client's lap, chitchatting. She tried to milk another dance out of him, but his wallet had apparently gotten thin—he declined. When the money ran out, Jade was gone.

I flagged her down.

"Hey, darlin'," she said with a sultry smile. She had the most delightful Texas drawl. "You ready for some company?"

"Indeed I am," I said.

The stunning vixen fell into my lap, wrapped an arm around me, and tried to hypnotize me with her mesmerizing green eyes. They were certainly eyes that had cast more than a few spells on unsuspecting men. She felt warm and soft in my lap, and her perfume filled my nostrils. It wouldn't take much convincing to part with my hard-earned cash. I could see why Paul Brown had been so enthralled with her.

"You fellows from out of town?"

"No. We're local," I said. "We're in here quite often. I'm surprised you don't recognize us."

Her eyes narrowed at me, and she looked at JD. "You're the singer for that band."

JD smiled.

She looked at me again. "You, I don't know you. But I think I'd like to."

It was a routine that she used on every client, but she made it sound like it was the first time those words ever crossed her plump lips.

Jade was the kind of girl that could make you reevaluate your priorities. Her sweet voice was like candy, and her svelte legs shimmered under the lights. It didn't take much imagination to picture coming home to that every day. Her every glance smoldered with possibilities, and it was a wonder that the very fabric on her skin didn't spontaneously combust. There was something about the way she bit her bottom lip and batted her eyelashes. She knew exactly what her gaze could do to a man. And like everyone who was in my position, I wanted to believe for an instant that she was sitting in my lap because she liked me.

But I knew better, and the fantasy had to end.

I reached into my pocket and pulled out my shiny gold badge. It sparkled as a stage light flashed across it.

Surprisingly, Jade was unfazed. "I love a man in uniform." Her green eyes surveyed me. "Now, you're not quite in uniform, are you?"

I whispered in her ear, "I'm undercover."

She giggled appropriately. It was all an act.

But it was an act I enjoyed at the moment. "I need to ask you a few questions."

"You can ask me anything you want," she said in a velvety voice.

I showed her a picture of Paul.

"Oh, I love Paul. He's not in any trouble, is he?"

"He's in a little bit of trouble."

She made a pouty face. "I hope it's not serious?"

"We think he was murdered."

She gasped. "Really? Paul was such a nice guy. Who would do that?"

"We were hoping you might be able to help us figure that out?"

"How would I be able to do that?

27

"I only saw him in the club," Jade said. "We didn't go on *'dates,'*" she said in air quotes.

"But he came in a lot," I said.

She nodded. "He was always in. Mostly with clients. But sometimes alone."

"You were his favorite."

She smiled. "He didn't see anyone else when he came in here."

"Why would he want to," I flirted.

"Exactly."

"You two saw each other on a regular basis. Spent a lot of time together. There must have been some type of relationship."

She shrugged. "Sure. I considered him a friend in that client kind of way. But nothing sexual. I wasn't attracted to him."

"Did you tell him that?"

"I'm not a fool. This is fantasy, dear. We all know the score."

"Do you think he was in love with you?"

"I think he had some kind of love for me. He talked about leaving his wife. I never encouraged him to do that."

"So he confided in you about his personal life."

"Yeah. Lotta guys come in here, and surprisingly, they just want to talk. Nobody listens to them. Their wives don't listen to them. They can't confess their deepest, darkest secrets to their friends. The girls in here are safe. You can say anything, and we don't judge. We just take your money. Kind of like a therapist, but more fun."

"Did he ever mention any personal problems? Any trouble? Any debts?"

"Oh, yeah, he had a lot of issues. I mean, where do you want me to start?"

"Wherever you feel comfortable."

"This could take a while, and the meter is running."

I grinned and dug into my pocket for my money clip. I peeled off a crisp $20 and handed it to her. She took it gratefully, and stuffed it into her high-heeled shoe.

"Well, he was in a sexless marriage. I don't know if it was exactly sexless per se, but he wasn't exactly thrilled with her performance, if you know what I mean. Maybe she wasn't thrilled with his performance, either. I think it happens to a lot of couples. They just get bored with each other. They lose that spark."

"I can't imagine anybody losing that spark with you."

"You're a smooth talker, aren't you?"

I smiled and shrugged.

"Did he ever mention the name Kim Gardner?"

"Yeah, he talked about her a few times. Brought her into the club once with some other clients. As I recall, the girl liked to have fun."

"Do you know if they were having a sexual relationship?"

"Yeah, he bragged about it a lot. I think he wanted me to know that he could get other women. You know, trying to make me jealous. Of course, I played the part."

"What about any other trouble? Debts?"

"He made it sound like he had a lot of money. And he certainly wasn't shy about spending it either, though I think he charged most of it on the company card. A lot of guys take clients here to sweeten the deal. I like to think we're responsible for keeping the business world running." She thought for a moment. "You know, I do remember one time, Paul getting a little uncomfortable when Freddy Fingers came into the club. They had a few words, and Freddy wasn't happy with him. I got the impression that he owed Freddy some money. Paul assured him that he would get it to him and that he was about to come into a windfall, as he had just closed a deal. Apparently, the bonus would be pretty large."

"Who's Freddy Fingers?"

"You two are cops, and you don't know?"

"Enlighten us."

Jade glanced around the club to see if anybody was in earshot. With the loud music and the visual distractions, no one was paying any attention to us, and our voices didn't carry in this environment.

"Freddy is connected."

"Mafia?"

Jade nodded. "I don't know his business, and I don't want to know. I just know that when he comes into the club, he's always with a couple of meatheads, and everybody seems afraid of him." She muttered aside, "From what I hear, he likes to cut off people's fingers."

"You know his real name?"

She shook her head.

"Thank you. This has been helpful."

She smiled. "I aim to please."

"You ready for that dance now?" She paused. "After all, you did pay me."

"I thought that was for the conversation."

"Maybe I'm feeling generous."

Who was I to say no?

28

W e stayed at *Forbidden Fruit* for a dance or two... or five. Jade was a talented girl with all the right moves. It was hard to leave, and the desire for a repeat performance was strong.

JD found a lovely young lady to lighten his wallet as well.

The sun angled toward the horizon, casting amber rays down the avenue as we stepped out of the dim establishment.

"Well, I'd say that was truly enlightening," JD said. "We learned a lot."

At least, that's what we told ourselves.

The crowd of tourists grew thicker as we strolled down the sidewalk to *Wetsuit*. JD wanted to grab a few appetizers and catch the end of their happy hour.

We passed by an alley, and I saw a homeless guy in a Santa costume sleeping on a mattress of cardboard. He didn't have the hat and the beard, just the pants. The jacket lay nearby. He wore an old pair of ratty sneakers.

I stepped into the alley to give him a closer look. It smelled like urine mixed with spoiled chicken, and as I got closer to the homeless guy, he didn't smell much better. There was an empty whiskey bottle by the lump of newsprint that was his pillow.

"Hey, buddy," I said.

He peeled open an eye and squinted at me. Through a few missing teeth, he barked, "The fuck do you want?"

This wasn't our guy. No way he was making phone calls over encrypted internet protocols.

"Where did you get the Santa suit?"

"I found it. What business is it of yours?"

I flashed my badge.

"Big tough policeman gonna arrest me?"

"Nope. You know you can go to the shelter, get a hot meal and a roof over your head?"

"Fuck the shelter. They got a curfew, and they don't take too kindly to my whiskey."

"When was the last time you had something to eat?"

He shrugged.

"Stick around, and I'll bring you a burger."

"With cheese, no mayo. I can't stand mayo."

"Anything else?"

"Six pack of beer and a bottle of Jack Daniels."

I chuckled. "Sorry. Just the food."

We left the alley, and I stopped in *Reefers* and ordered a cheeseburger to go.

It took 15 minutes for the kitchen to grill up the burger. They handed it to me in a cardboard to-go box and tossed extra ketchup and mustard into the bag at my request.

I delivered the meal, along with a soda. I don't think my new friend in the alley was too concerned about dental hygiene or cavities. He accepted the meal with a dose of skepticism. "You didn't spit in this, did you?"

I laughed. "No."

"I don't have to do anything for this, do I?"

"No. A gift from one human being to another. Enjoy. What's your name?"

"Carl."

"Nice to meet you, Carl."

We left him to his meal and continued on our journey to *Wetsuit.*

"Don't worry," JD said. "I won't tell anybody you're a nice guy."

"I wouldn't want to ruin my reputation."

We grabbed our usual seat at a high-top table near the bar, and a delightful young waitress named Crystal served us.

I called my friend Tony Scarpetti. He was an old Mafia-type that had gone legitimate—well, mostly legitimate. He still ran a high-stakes poker game at the *Seven Seas*. It was THE card game on the island and saw an eclectic mix of players —everyone from politicians to gangsters. And there never was much difference between the two. Tony also ran a couple of restaurants and had the best pizza in town. If anybody could tell me about Freddy Fingers, it would be Tony.

"Freddy Antonini. Yeah, I know the guy."

"What's he into?"

"You know, a little of this, a little of that."

"Murder, extortion, racketeering?" I suggested.

"Along with gambling, loansharking, money laundering, and whatever else will make a buck. Why? What are you interested in him for?"

"Potential suspect in the death of Paul Brown. I'm told he owed Freddy Fingers money."

"A lot of people owe Freddy money. A lot of people lose their fingers if they're late on payments."

"You know where I can find him?"

"He owns that joint on Willet Avenue. Bella Ragazza."

"Thanks for the info."

"Anytime." He paused. "Don't stir up too much trouble. He's not a nice guy."

"You know me. Do I ever stir up trouble?"

Tony laughed.

We chowed on appetizers, sipped fine whiskey, and watched the restaurant fill up with pretty people. Afterward, we went to *Tide Pool* and continued our indulgences, watching pert assets frolicking in the outdoor pool.

To my surprise, I saw Alexandria in the water, wearing a skimpy red bikini that looked painted on. She batted around an oversized beach ball with one hand, making sure to keep her cocktail out of the water with the other. She was surrounded by a couple of young, hunky guys in their mid 20s.

"I think we have a bonafide cougar," JD said.

"In the wild," I added.

She looked just as good in a bikini as I had imagined she would.

We sipped our whiskey and watched her flirt with the boys. She could have her pick.

She didn't notice us until she climbed out of the water, her smooth skin beading up, the red bikini—almost translucent now—clinging to her curves. She toweled off and sauntered in our direction after one of her boy-toys brought her another drink. "Deputies. Surprised to see you here."

"I could say the same. I take it you are enjoying your evening."

"I am."

The pretty boys hovered nearby, giving us dirty looks.

"We talked to an informant who claims Paul admitted to having an affair with Kim Gardner."

Alexandria shrugged. "Love flourishes where it wants."

"You don't seem too concerned."

"It doesn't matter now, does it?"

"No. But it certainly does give Kevin Gardner motive," I said.

"Gives Linda Brown motive, too," JD added.

She thought for a moment. "I guess it's possible that either one of them could have slipped out of sight, attacked Paul, and pushed him overboard. But there were people all over the boat. Mostly on the aft deck or in the salon. There were people milling about on the foredeck and the sky deck. Somebody would have seen something." She thought for another moment. "I heard something about a wine bottle. Perhaps Paul was standing by the gunwale, and someone struck him. It wouldn't take much to shove him overboard, and if it happened quickly, it might have gone unnoticed."

"I think that's a possibility. But I'm also beginning to think that maybe he was struck below deck in a stateroom."

"And how did he get overboard?"

"Not sure," I said.

"Someone would have had to drag him into the companionway and hoist the body over while he was unconscious. Seems unlikely. And the boat was searched multiple times."

"It was just a thought," I said.

Her boy-toys grew impatient.

"Let's do shots," the dark-haired one said.

"Totally," the blond agreed.

"How about you boys go do your shots while I continue my conversation with the deputies," Alexandria said. "Put it on my tab."

They gave her annoyed glances.

"Run along," she said, flicking them away with her hand.

They reluctantly complied and headed toward the tiki bar to order.

Alexandria pulled up a chair and took a seat. She leaned back, sipped her drink, and crossed her legs. She had nice legs.

"I also hear that Paul was into the mob for a considerable amount of money," I said.

"I don't know anything about that. But as far as I know, there weren't any Mafia members aboard my boat."

"Somebody killed him," I said flatly.

"Can you confirm that? I mean, this is still all just speculation."

"You're right. We haven't confirmed anything."

"Well, Deputy, you're more than welcome to come back to the boat and look over the scene once again and see if you can find any additional clues," she said with a flirty gaze. "I mean, we could go look right now."

"What about your *friends*?"

Her boy-toys were still at the tiki bar.

"They're fun to look at, but they're not quite stimulating me intellectually." Her sultry eyes sparkled.

29

We ended up back aboard her boat, strictly for investigational purposes, of course. She offered us a drink as we stepped into the salon, and it would be rude to decline.

She had put on a pair of jean shorts over her bikini bottoms before we left *Tide Pool*. We gave her a ride back to the marina in the Porsche. She liked the car, but this was a hard woman to impress. She could afford just about anything she wanted.

She slid behind the bar, filled glasses full of whiskey, then dealt them out. She lifted her glass to toast. "To Paul Brown."

We clinked glasses and echoed her sentiment.

"Any crew or staff aboard?"

"Why do you ask?"

"It's a big boat."

"I can manage. And I like my privacy. I only bring in staff for special occasions."

I took a sip of my drink, then asked, "Mind if I walk around?"

"Be my guest."

"You said the last place you saw Paul was in the forward passage near the day head."

"That's correct.

"Show me."

"Certainly." She stepped from behind the bar, then sauntered forward.

JD and I followed as her hips swayed from side to side. She led us down the passage to the day head.

"I was standing right here. I had just come across from the galley, checking with the staff to make sure we had enough hors d'oeuvres and alcohol. We chatted for a bit, and I admonished his behavior. I feel bad because I wasn't too friendly about it. I was quite upset."

Forward of the day head was the VIP stateroom. A cross companionway led to the stairs and the galley on the port side.

I moved forward and pushed out the receiving entrance onto the starboard side deck and glanced around. The forensics guys had gone over this entire boat with a fine-tooth comb. But they hadn't sprayed Luminol—a chemiluminescence agent that reacts with blood and fluoresces briefly.

I tried to imagine a potential scenario playing out on the side deck. The waves gently lapped against the hull, and the moonlight shimmered the water. The marina was calm and peaceful. But the echo of murder lingered, and only the bulkheads knew the truth.

We stepped back into the passageway.

"I'm getting out of these wet clothes," Alexandria said. "You boys feel free to look anywhere you like."

She sauntered down the forward passage to the master stateroom and opened the hatch. She stepped inside and immediately pulled the string on her bikini top. The skimpy fabric fell free. She tossed it aside and began to shimmy out of her shorts and bikini bottoms at the same time in full view. She knew we could see her, and I think she liked it.

She never bothered to close the hatch.

We were perfect gentlemen and didn't steal more than one or two glances before forcing ourselves to maintain some degree of professionalism. We walked back into the salon.

JD whispered, "Maybe I should leave you here to investigate things alone. She seems to have taken an interest in you."

"She's a suspect in a crime."

"Well, the real crime is going to be if you don't give her a thorough interrogation." He raised his hands innocently. "Just saying."

"Believe me, it's tempting."

"I know, I know. Professional ethics. But one can dream, right?"

"What are you boys whispering about?" Alexandria said as she returned to the salon wearing a sheer black négligée. She might as well have been wearing nothing at all.

We both swallowed hard and tried to look unimpressed. We failed miserably.

"Do you mind if we come back tomorrow with a forensics team?" I asked. "If Paul was struck over the head, perhaps we could find some blood evidence here."

"You're more than welcome to look. But I had the boat cleaned since the party. She cringed. "Should I not have done that?"

"It would have been best not to."

"I didn't think it was important at the time. I'm kind of obsessive about my space. It has to be clean, especially after having people over."

"It's not a problem."

JD said, "He could have just fallen off the starboard side, gotten sucked under the boat, bumped his head, and missed the propellers."

"Maybe it's that simple," I said.

"Maybe not," Alexandria said. "Something tells me you've got good gut instincts. Your gut instinct is telling you he was killed aboard this boat. I think you should go with that."

JD looked at his watch, then patted me on the back. "Well, I'm about to turn into a pumpkin, but you should stay here and discuss possibilities with Ms. West."

I scowled at him.

"Yes, I'd love that."

"Another night, perhaps," I said. "Professional responsibility. You understand."

She lifted an intrigued eyebrow. "What do you think will happen if your friend leaves you here alone with me?"

I knew exactly what she wanted to happen.

"I wouldn't want anybody to get the wrong impression."

"I can keep a secret if you can."

"You like to flirt with danger, don't you, Ms. West?"

She smiled. "Are you dangerous, Mr. Wild?" she asked, strolling toward me, stalking me like prey.

I smirked. "Given the right situations."

She was close now. So close I could smell the chlorine on her skin from the pool. That négligée was extremely sheer.

She sighed. "I understand. I wouldn't want you to get in trouble. Perhaps we can take a raincheck on the stimulating discussion?"

I played it cool. "Perhaps."

She was a stimulating woman.

"Thanks for the ride home, gentlemen."

"Thanks for the drinks," I said.

"Just let me know when you want to take a closer look," she said, catching my eyes inadvertently dropping to her buoyant, stimulated endowments.

I'm sure she was talking about the crime scene.

30

"If you don't get on that after this investigation is over, I am," JD said on the ride home.

"Trust me, I will give that serious consideration," I replied.

He dropped me off at the marina, and I told him we'd catch up in the morning. He zipped away, the engine howling into the night as I hustled down the dock to the *Avventura*. The stars were out in full force, and there was hardly a cloud in the sky.

I crossed the passerelle to the aft deck, and Buddy greeted me at the salon door. I leashed him up and took him out for a walk before crawling into bed with thoughts of missed opportunities. But that would have been more trouble than it was worth. At least, that's what I kept telling myself as I tried not to think about sheer black négligées.

Daniels called sometime before dawn. My phone buzzed incessantly on the nightstand, and it took me a moment to realize that I should probably answer it. My hand snatched the device, and I swiped the screen. It was pitch black outside. I scratched out the words, "What is it?"

"It's a nightmare. That's what it is."

I groaned.

"That sicko Santa Claus struck again."

I cringed. "Where?"

"Taffy Beach."

"What exactly happened?"

"You'll see when you get here. Call numb-nuts and get here right away."

I ended the call, dialed JD, and the phone went straight to voicemail.

I pulled myself out of bed, wiped the sleep from my eyes, and hopped into the shower.

I gave Jack another call after I'd gotten dressed. He finally answered with a groggy, annoyed voice. "You better be calling to tell me you went back over there and *investigated* Ms. West."

"Not exactly."

I filled him in on the situation.

"Does Daniels know what time it is?"

"It's 3:45 AM."

"This is criminal."

"Maybe we should just ban murders between the hours of midnight and 8 AM," I said dryly.

"That would be a good start."

"Are you getting out of bed, or am I handling this one alone?"

"I'm up," he said like a zombie.

"I'll call you back in five minutes, just to be sure."

"No need."

He hung up, and I hustled down to the galley and ate a bowl of cereal. I was out of breakfast burritos and had no time to fix a proper meal.

I called JD back.

"I'm on my way," he assured.

"You haven't left the house yet."

"I know, but I'm up. That's a start."

He showed up 15 minutes later, and we zipped to Taffy Beach and pulled into the parking lot. Brenda and the forensics guys were there. Red and blues from patrol cars flickered.

We hopped out and hustled down the beach to join the crew of first responders. There were a couple of people standing around gawking at the charred remains of two victims—one male, one female. At first glance, they looked like wood that had been in a fire—charred black, ashen, split and cracked like a dry lake bed.

The putrid stench of burnt flesh filled the air, and wisps of smoke still wafted from the remains.

"Do we know what happened?" I asked the sheriff as we arrived on the scene.

Sheriff Daniels pointed to a young couple standing nearby. They were in their early 20s. "They stumbled across the remains."

"Did they see anything?"

"They said they were in the parking lot when they heard two pops and saw muzzle flash. They said a guy wearing a Santa costume torched the couple on the beach, then took off across Ocean Avenue."

"Yeah, the whole thing was crazy," the guy said, holding his girl's hand. "Honestly, we were both stunned."

"We stayed in the car for a minute until he took off," the girl added. "I don't want to sound callous, but I didn't want to get anywhere near that guy. As soon as he left, we got out of the car and ran down the beach."

"Did you see where he went?"

The guy pointed to the boulevard. "He crossed Ocean Avenue and disappeared into an alley."

"This is the same guy from Fort Dawson, isn't it?" the girl asked excitedly.

"Most likely," I said. I thanked them for the info and asked Daniels, "Anybody else see anything?"

"If they did, they aren't saying. Looks like the victims were fooling around on the beach when Kris Kringle decided to pay them a visit."

Brenda hovered over the smoldering remains, wearing nitrile gloves. "Entry wound is in the male's back and another in the female's chest. He shot them and torched them before they had an opportunity to react."

"Any shell casings?" I asked.

She gave a cursory glance around the surrounding area, and I snapped on a pair of gloves, squatted down, and sifted through the sand. JD did as well.

After a few moments, JD exclaimed, "Got one!" A grin tugged his lips. "9mm. He must have missed this one. Getting sloppy."

"I'll see if there are any security cameras in the area that may have caught a glimpse of our perp," I said.

The inky black waves crashed against the shore, and the stars glimmered above. I walked up the beach, climbed the berm to the sidewalk, and crossed Ocean Avenue. There was hardly any traffic at this hour. A row of storefronts lined the boulevard—a Quick Mart, a T-shirt shop, a surf shop, and a few eateries. There was an ATM in the Quik Mart, but it was facing away from the street, and its camera wouldn't have captured anything. I knew the store had security cameras aimed at the door and at the product aisles, but those weren't likely to have caught anything either.

I hustled along the storefronts, looking for any security cameras that might have caught an angle on the crime.

I didn't see any.

I pushed into the alley that the witnesses said the perp escaped through. It was littered with paper and debris, large green lawn and leaf bags, and a dumpster. An orange mercury vapor light buzzed overhead, casting long shadows. Nobody was sleeping in this alley.

I exited the passage a block over and gave a look around.

The street was empty—a few cars parked at the curb.

No witnesses here.

The perp had probably slipped into a nearby neighborhood. Maybe he dashed away in a car parked on a side street. Or maybe he walked all the way home.

The deputies would canvas the area after daybreak, knocking on doors, looking for footage from video doorbells and neighborhood security cams.

31

The sky faded from black to lavender. Then the amber ball inched above the horizon, eviscerating the night for good, painting the tangerine sky.

We caught a break.

Sort of.

The perp had tripped a motion detector on the video doorbell of a resident in a nearby neighborhood.

That was the good news.

The bad news was that it was a first-generation camera—black and white with poor lowlight capabilities. The footage was super grainy and wasn't in high def. But there was no mistaking the Wicked Santa, complete with a blowtorch, trotting down the street. He hopped into what looked like a black Mustang parked at the curb. Santa climbed behind the wheel, cranked up the engine, and drove away.

The homeowner exported the file, and we gave it to the nerd herd to see if they could sharpen the image and pull a plate number from the vehicle.

At the department, JD and I grabbed a cup of fresh coffee, and I asked Denise to look up registration records for every black or midnight blue Mustang on the island. "Better include dark brown and lapis green," I said. The black and white footage made it impossible to judge color.

"That could be a pretty broad search," she said.

"It's a start."

"You know what I think," JD said.

I looked at him, waiting for him to reveal a grand theory.

"I think that I need to get a proper breakfast. I say we go to Waffle Wizard."

"Bring me back peanut butter waffles," Denise said.

"I believe we can accommodate that request," JD replied.

She shrugged. "I'm just kinda craving one right now."

We left the department and headed to the *Waffle Wizard*. A hostess that looked like she'd been on shift all night seated us in a booth by the window.

The restaurant had that classic diner vibe. Blue vinyl booths, a checkered tile floor, a waffle bar with fixed bar stools that spun 360°. There was a jukebox in the corner and a large statue of the Waffle Wizard outside. You could get milkshakes, chocolate sundaes, banana splits, root beer floats, and whatever other kind of sugary delight you could imagine. Its main competition on the island was *Waffle*

World, and the two had a lot of similarities. The Wizard had chocolate waffles, peanut butter waffles, blueberry, strawberry, pecan, almond, and the list went on. If Waffle World added a new variety, the Wizard followed and vice versa.

JD ordered blueberry waffles with a fried egg, bacon, and hash browns. I went for the jumbo French toast with hash browns and bacon. It didn't take long for our meal to arrive. JD slathered his waffles with butter and syrup, and we feasted like kings, hoping the high-calorie meal would make up for the lack of sleep and excessive alcohol.

It didn't.

I ordered peanut butter waffles to go for Denise. The meal included bacon and two pieces of toast with a side of jelly.

With full bellies, we paid the tab and headed back to the Sheriff's Office. Denise was mighty appreciative when we dropped off breakfast. "I can't eat like this all the time. But every now and then is not going to kill me."

"I don't think you have anything to worry about," I said. She had a perfect little figure and somehow seemed to make the polyester uniform a thing of beauty.

Brenda called as we were about to leave. "Preliminary toxicology report came back on Paul Brown. You're going to love this."

32

"It's looking like not only was Paul Brown bashed over the head, he was poisoned," Brenda said.

"With what?"

"Ethylene glycol. It's colorless, odorless, and tastes sweet. He would appear intoxicated at the initial onset of symptoms. I guess it wasn't working fast enough for our killer's liking."

"Or more than one person wanted him dead."

"That's a possibility."

"Thanks for the info."

"My pleasure."

I ended the call and caught JD up to speed.

"I think we need to expand our minds. We've been focusing on party guests, but you know who we've ignored?"

"Waitstaff," I said.

"Bingo."

"Would have been easy to slip something in a beverage."

"We've been assuming that he was struck and dumped overboard right away," I said. "What if he was still on board when we searched?"

"We looked over every inch of that ship," JD said.

"The catering crew brought equipment, serving trays, carts, and waste containers."

JD followed along. "He could have been stuffed into a bin or a bag and removed with the staff."

"Then dumped in the water later."

"Why?"

I shrugged. "West-Tek is a defense company. I can think of a dozen reasons why someone might want Paul Brown dead."

"I've dug into the waitstaff that was onboard," Denise said. "There were a couple of students. Mostly the staff was full-time service industry personnel. Some have other jobs at bars and restaurants. The manager that night, Vanessa Santini, has been on staff with Coconut Catering for the last 10 years. None of them had any criminal history. I mean, traffic tickets and moving violations, but nothing major."

"Dig into them a little closer."

"I'm on it."

"I think it's time we re-interview some of the waitstaff," JD said. "I know they were all questioned the night of Paul's disappearance, but let's see if we can drum up any inconsistencies."

We left the station and strolled across the parking lot to the orange beast. I texted Isabella with the names of the wait-staff that were onboard the *War Games* that evening. [See if you can connect any of these people to West-Tek.]

We hopped into the convertible, and Jack cranked up the engine. We pulled out of the lot and were heading toward the catering company's headquarters when Denise called. "That catering company is owned by Coconut Catering Unlimited, LLC, which is owned by a guy named Freddy Antonini."

My brow lifted with surprise. "Really?"

"Name sound familiar?"

"It does. Thank you. You're amazing."

"I know."

The catering company was located next door to *Bella Ragazza* on Willet Avenue. I should have put the two together sooner. Bella Ragazza supplied all the food.

We found a place to park and pushed into the restaurant. Bella Ragazza smelled like Italian seasoning, mozzarella, and zesty red sauce.

Denise had texted me a photo of Freddy, and I saw him sitting in a booth at the back of the restaurant, seated across the table from one of his minions.

Freddie was a thick bruiser in his mid 50s. He had a hard, square face that was lined and a nose that had been flat-tened by more than a few fists back in the day. He was a little thicker in the midsection than when he was in his prime, but he looked like he could still handle himself well. Freddy was dressed in a gray sharkskin *Amadori* suit and tie. There was a half-eaten plate of lasagna in front of him and a glass of red wine.

I flashed my badge as we reached the booth. "I hate to interrupt your meal, but I need to ask you a few questions."

The muscle-head across the table from Freddy was mid 30s. His long, dark hair was pulled into a tight ponytail. His tight black t-shirt stretched against his thick chest and arms. He glared at us, full of contempt. It looked like he was about to stand up and get in our faces, but Freddy waved him off.

"What can I do for you, Deputies?" Freddy asked in a pleasant tone.

"You know a guy named Paul Brown?"

"Never heard of him."

"That's interesting. I hear he owes you money. *Owed* you money. He's not around anymore. Went missing from a yacht that your company was catering. He was poisoned."

"That's terrible. What's that got to do with me?"

"You don't find that odd?"

"My company does a lot of catering."

"Do a lot of people die after your company serves them food?"

His face tightened, and his pleasant demeanor was on the verge of evaporating. "Are you suggesting he was poisoned by one of my staff?"

I shrugged.

"That's nonsense."

"So, you didn't have anything to do with Paul Brown's death?"

"Why would I make somebody disappear that supposedly owes me money?"

I shrugged. "I thought you didn't know the guy."

Freddie smiled. "I'm just saying, your logic doesn't make sense."

"Maybe you figured Paul wasn't good for the money. Maybe you wanted to send a message."

Freddie chuckled. "I think you're letting your imagination run away with you. I'm a businessman. And I'm very careful about who I do business with. The people I loan money to always pay me back."

"They'd be stupid not to."

He stared at me for a long moment. "It's been nice chatting with you, but I'd like to get back to my meal."

"Of course."

"Feel free to grab a table. Your meal is on the house."

"Thank you," I said. "Some other time."

We left the restaurant, and JD muttered, "You didn't expect him to talk, did you?"

"No. But maybe we rattled his cage."

We stopped in the catering company and spoke with the manager, Vanessa Santini. She was on the phone at her desk when we entered. Staff scurried about prepping for an upcoming gig. Vanessa ended the call shortly after I flashed my badge. "Deputies, what can I do for you?"

"We'd like to follow up with you about Paul Brown," I said.

"I already told the deputies everything I know, but I'm happy to answer any questions you may have."

"Ethylene glycol was found in his system."

Vanessa's face crinkled. "What's that?"

"A common ingredient in antifreeze."

Her eyes widened. "How would antifreeze get into his system?"

"That's what we're trying to figure out. Did you or any of the staff know the deceased?"

"I never met the man before in my life. I can't speak for my staff, but nobody mentioned anything."

"I hear your boss might have known him."

"You'd have to ask Mr. Antonini about that."

"He denies any relationship."

"Well, there you go."

"How much of the day-to-day operations does Freddy oversee?"

"Very little. He lets me run the business, and I think I've done a pretty damn good job over the last decade."

"Did you see anyone slip anything into Paul Brown's drink that evening?"

"As I recall, Mr. Brown had quite a lot to drink that evening."

"Poisoning with ethylene glycol can mimic intoxication. He might not have been as drunk as he appeared."

"I didn't see anything, but in all honesty, my focus was elsewhere."

I recognized a few staff members that had worked the yacht party. "Mind if I ask your staff additional questions?"

"I'd prefer you do that on their personal time. We have an event that we're prepping for now. I can't really spare the time. I can give you a list of all personnel that was aboard Ms. West's yacht that evening, but I'm sure you already have that."

I nodded.

"I'm sorry I can't be of more assistance. If you have any additional questions, please don't hesitate to get in contact."

I thanked her for her time, and we left the establishment.

"None of those employees have a record," JD said. "Murder seems like a big jump."

"People do strange things for money."

"But why use an amateur?"

I shrugged.

"Surely, if Freddy Fingers wanted Paul Brown dead, he could have gotten to him other ways."

We hopped into the Porsche and headed to Big Tony's Pizza. The waffles we had for breakfast didn't last long, and the aroma of Italian food got me thinking about cheesy goodness.

We grabbed a couple slices and chowed down in a booth. Tony wasn't around, but we never had to pay at Big Tony's, even though we tried. We'd done Tony a favor in the past, and that favor would last for life.

I got an anonymous call as we finished up. I swiped the screen and held the device to my ear. "This is Deputy Wild. How can I help you?"

33

"I have pertinent information about Paul Brown," the woman said.

I didn't recognize the timid voice. "What kind of information?"

"I don't want to talk over the phone. Call me paranoid, but after what I've seen, I'm not taking any chances."

"What's your name?"

"Is there somewhere we can meet?"

"No safer place than the Sheriff's Department," I said.

"No. I want to remain anonymous. I'll talk to you, and only you. I don't think you're fully aware of what's going on or how big this really is."

"Okay. Where do you want to meet?"

"Someplace out of public view. I'm afraid if somebody sees me talking to you, I could be next."

"Okay."

"There's a warehouse not far from where all those crappy bands practice. Do you know the place?"

I chuckled. "I know the place."

"I could meet you there in 20 minutes."

"Okay."

"Good. I look forward to it."

"How will I know you?"

"I'll be the only one there."

She ended the call, and I forwarded the number to Isabella. [Can you track that number?]

I didn't get an immediate reply. Isabella had better things to do than jump every time I called. She ran one of the most powerful clandestine agencies in the world and dealt with problems far more urgent than local homicides.

I filled JD in on the details. After we scarfed down the last bites of pizza, we left Big Tony's and drove toward the warehouse district. It only took a few minutes to get there, so JD pulled into the parking lot of the practice studio to kill time before our meeting.

A band rumbled inside, the snap of the snare drum echoing across the lot. We hopped out of the car and strolled toward the entrance. The usual group of miscreants hung outside, drinking beer and smoking cigarettes. At this point, they didn't even bother to toss the joints.

They high-fived Jack as we passed by, and we pushed into the dim hallway. The walls vibrated as guitars thundered and basses boomed. A slightly off-pitch singer howled into a microphone.

JD pulled the keys from his pocket as he stood at the door to *Wild Fury's* practice space. He'd left a pair of sunglasses atop Dizzy's amp.

He twisted the key, but the action was surprisingly light. The door hadn't been locked.

No cause for alarm. Maybe a band member was inside.

Jack pushed open the door, and a slew of expletives launched from his mouth. You could barely hear his scream over the rumble of the neighboring band.

My jaw dropped when I looked inside, and my eyes rounded. My hands balled into fists, my teeth clenched tight.

The space was empty.

Totally empty.

Styxx's candy-apple red drum set with double bass and cymbals—gone. Dizzy's Marshall stack and guitars—gone. Crash's booming bass rig—gone. The PA system with a power amp, mixing board, and massive speakers had vanished. The thieves had left nothing but the ratty old couch in the corner.

Jack looked like he was about to explode. And I couldn't blame him. His cheeks were tomato red, and the veins in his temples pulsed. "Who left the door unlocked? Who was the last person in here?"

"I don't think anybody left the door unlocked," I said, pointing to the wall. Someone had cut out a square in the drywall with a Sawzall large enough for a person to fit through. They'd been kind enough to replace the square, but that was the end of their generosity. I pulled it out, revealing a passageway into the neighboring practice room.

It was empty as well, and there were holes in the walls in the neighboring studio where the thieves had done the same thing. They gained access to one room, then carved their way into the others and absconded with tens of thousands of dollars worth of equipment during the night. This wasn't like having a guitar stolen at a gig. This was a professional operation.

We didn't have time for this right now. And with the upcoming show, this put the band in a bind.

I stepped into the hallway and examined the door to the neighboring unit. It looked undisturbed. I twisted the handle, and the door opened. It wasn't locked. My guess was that somebody just forgot. It was blind luck that the thieves had stumbled across an open door. But maybe they had been casing out the joint, checking every day, looking for opportunities.

Everyone on the island in *the scene* knew this was home to dozens of bands. There were no security systems in the practice spaces. No security cameras in the parking lot. The building owner had no intention of going to the added expense. And even if he did, the cameras wouldn't last a day before being vandalized. This wasn't the kind of crowd that wanted to be actively monitored.

We turned a blind eye to a lot of things that went on around the warehouse. Musicians and illicit drugs go hand-in-hand, but we had bigger fish to fry than busting a rock band for a quarter-ounce of weed, which the DA had stopped prosecuting. Such activities wouldn't endear us to our neighbors, either.

JD finally stopped grumbling. He locked up the studio—not that it did much good—and we headed outside to talk to the miscreants.

"You guys see anybody roll out of here with a ton of equipment?" I asked.

They all exchanged glances.

"No, why? You guys get ripped off again?"

"Yeah, and a few others."

"That's fucked up," the kid said.

"Deputies will be here shortly to evaluate the situation. Be cooperative with them."

"Right on."

I didn't worry about the miscreants. They were harmless. I knew that if they turned out their pockets, I might find something. A joint. A few pills, maybe. But nothing worth hassling with. They certainly weren't stealing equipment. These kids were here day-in, day-out, rain or shine. This was their social circle. They weren't about to shit where they ate.

I called Sheriff Daniels, informed him of the situation, and asked him to send Mendoza and Robinson over, along with the forensics team.

JD and I hopped into the Porsche and drove a couple blocks to the abandoned warehouse for our meeting.

The old four-story red brick building had been standing

since the turn of the century. It was dilapidated, and had seen more than its share of nefarious activity. The windows were milky and cracked, some of them knocked out completely. Quite often, people would take potshots at the building.

Sometimes kids would party there. At other times, a home-less person would curl up for the night. Criminals had used it as a rendezvous point. It had quite an illustrious history.

A chain-link fence, topped with razor wire, surrounded the area. But the fence was in disrepair, and the gate had been damaged and was no longer in existence. You could freely enter and exit the lot. There were several blue steel bins that people had used to make bonfires in, and there was a heap of trash and debris by the loading dock.

I looked at my watch as we pulled in. There were no other cars inside the enclosure. It was time to meet our informant. Perhaps she hadn't arrived yet. We waited in the car for another minute, listening to the stereo.

Still, no one turned up.

For an instant, I thought our informant got cold feet.

Jack killed the engine, and we hopped out of the car. We climbed the stairs to the loading dock that was overgrown with weeds sprouting through the cracks in the pavement.

"Shit," I muttered under my breath, realizing that my phone had slipped from my pocket.

I spun around and darted back down the steps to the car to grab it. I knew better than to leave a phone in a car in this neighborhood. It wouldn't be there by the time I got back, even though we were going to be close by.

I leaned over the door and reached down. My fingers snatched the device that was perched by the seat bolster. I slipped it in my pocket and turned around to jog back up the steps.

JD was already at the main door. Over the years, the lock had been broken. People had pried the door open. Several of the transom windows were slightly ajar. Access to the building was easy. I wasn't totally sure who owned it at this point in time, but nobody seemed to care. It changed hands a few times in the last decade, with each new owner intending to renovate it, bring it up to code, and turn it into luxury apartments or some other manifestation. But it didn't take long for them to find out the project was a nightmare. The historic building was loaded with asbestos and in dire need of remediation, making the cost to bring it back to life exorbitant. I guess the numbers just hadn't made sense yet to anyone.

Even if a developer turned it into condos, you were pioneering in this area. It wasn't really the place to be after dark.

JD grabbed the handle and started to pull open the steel door.

That's when it happened.

34

The deafening blast echoed across the concrete, bouncing off the brick walls of other buildings. The ground rumbled underfoot, and even at a distance, the overpressure knocked me off my feet. The amber blast flickered for an instant, blowing the steel door from its hinges and sending JD soaring through the air off the loading dock.

Bits of blistering shrapnel sprayed in all directions. Smoke and haze filled the air.

The blast muted the world for a moment.

Slowly, my hearing began to return, but my ears would ring for days.

Bits of brick-and-mortar scattered, raining down over the lot.

I gathered my wits and pushed off the ground, staggering to my feet. I scanned the haze for JD.

He lay on the ground 20 yards from the entrance. I sprinted to his aid. The rusty steel door was the only thing between him and death, and it had done a good job of keeping shrapnel from turning him into Swiss cheese.

JD was no spring chicken, and that was a long way to get hurled through the air. He was unconscious when I reached him. I took a cursory glance over his body, looking for signs of trauma.

Jack peeled open his eyes and groaned, "Son-of-a-bitch."

He tried to sit up, but that was a bad idea. Pain winced his face. He'd taken a pretty heavy impact, and the air had been knocked from his lungs.

I dialed 911 and shouted, "Officer down." I gave the operator the details of our location, and she stayed on the line. I told JD to take it easy. Help was on the way.

He lay on the asphalt, staring at the sky, trying to breathe— each breath labored.

"Wiggle your toes," I said.

His checkered Vans moved, and that was an indication that he probably didn't have a spinal cord injury.

After he caught his breath, he tried to sit up again. He groaned as I helped him up.

His elbows, back, and forearms were covered in road rash. Crimson blood seeped from his abrasions. "Remind me not to do that again."

I chuckled.

"Next time, you're going in first," he said.

EMTs, paramedics, and patrol units arrived shortly. The lights from an ambulance flickered, and the red and blues from patrol cars flashed. A fire truck arrived, and medical personnel attended to JD. They took his vital signs and asked simple questions to evaluate his cognitive abilities. "Do you know where you are?"

"Coconut Key."

"Do you know what day it is?"

"The day I should have stayed in bed."

JD was able to get on his feet after a while. The EMTs helped him hobble to the ambulance. They wanted to take him to the hospital for a full evaluation, and JD didn't protest. He dug into his pocket and tossed me the keys to the Porsche. There was no way he was leaving his brand-new car in the warehouse district with the top down.

An EMT closed the door to the ambulance, then hustled around to the passenger side and hopped in. The meat wagon pulled away and rushed JD to the emergency room.

Paris Delaney was on the scene with her crew. There were a few other channels there as well. She grabbed footage and gave a report with the chaos in the background.

Sheriff Daniels arrived, and we chatted for a moment. "Any idea who this supposed informant was?"

"No, but you can be damn sure I'll find out."

"You think the bomb was geared toward you two or the informant?"

I shrugged. "Hard to say, but I have a sneaking suspicion somebody doesn't like us digging into this case."

Bomb squad and arson investigators sifted through the rubble. It was a simple pipe bomb that was tripped by opening the door. It didn't take much to build one. Just some supplies from a hardware store—pipe, end caps, a battery, smokeless gunpowder, and ball bearings for extra lethality.

The ball bearings had been duct-taped around the outside of the device, creating dozens of tiny projectiles hungry for flesh. It was a particularly insidious construction. There's nothing friendly about a bomb, but when a bomb-maker goes to these lengths, it's plain sadistic.

Each bomb has a signature, and every bomb maker has a style. In their mind, they are creating works of art. Amateurs assume that the explosion will destroy all the evidence. But in reality, it creates more. I had no doubt the forensic investigators could pull some useful information from the construction materials.

Daniels groaned as Paris marched our way.

"Sheriff, do you have any idea who's responsible for the blast?"

"If I knew who was responsible, they'd be behind bars." He walked out of frame, done with the interview.

The camera, and Paris, focused on me. "Was Deputy Donovan the intended target?"

"Hard to say."

She told the camera guy to cut. It was a rare move for the ambitious blonde. "He's going to be okay, right?"

The camera and sound guy drifted away and grabbed more B-roll as investigators sifted through the debris.

"I think so."

"Wish him well for me," she said, genuine concern in her eyes.

"I will. Thank you."

She backed away and rejoined her crew.

I dialed the number of the anonymous tipster, but there was no answer.

My next call was to Isabella. I told her what had happened.

"Oh my God, is he all right?"

"I think he's gonna be fine. A little battered and bruised. Fortunately, he didn't have any puncture wounds."

"One of these days, you guys are going to run out of lives."

"Don't say that."

"All of you... Every single one... You think you're immortal."

"I know better."

"It catches up with all of us," she said.

"Are you trying to talk us into retirement?"

"I know better than that. Just be careful."

"Any information about the phone the tip was made from?"

"It's not on the grid right now. It's a prepaid cellular. When the call was made to your phone, your informant was already at the warehouse. I think it's safe to say that your informant may have placed the bomb."

"Good to know."

"You should vet your sources more carefully."

"I tried. You should have gotten back to me sooner."

"Sorry. Busy day at the office." She paused. "Keep me posted on JD."

"I will."

I ended the call and hopped into the Porsche. The bomb guys and arson investigators would be on the scene for quite some time, trying to collect every last bit of evidence.

I drove to the emergency room, and by that time, JD had been triaged, scanned, and was in a patient room. We had been in that place so many times by now we were on a first-name basis with the staff.

JD was propped up in bed with an IV dripping into his forearm, chatting with a cute nurse. A bedside monitor displayed his vitals, and he had changed into a pale green hospital gown with a diamond pattern.

"Is he gonna live?" I joked with the nurse.

"This one is too ornery to die," she said before darting out of the room.

"Dr. Parker thinks I have a mild concussion," JD said. "Maybe a couple of cracked ribs. I've got some pretty severe bruising, I'll tell you that. Waiting on the scan results."

"I'd say you got lucky."

"If I were lucky, I wouldn't have been anywhere near that warehouse. You find anything out about the tipster?"

I told him what Isabella told me.

Dr. Parker stepped into the room, and his annoyed eyes flicked between the two of us. His face tightened into a frown. "What do I have to do to keep you two out of here?"

JD pointed at me. "This is all his fault."

I raised my hands innocently.

"It was *your* informant," JD said. He asked Dr. Parker, "What's the damage?"

"My evaluation tells me that you're mentally defective."

JD frowned at him.

"But you're going to live. I don't know how, but you don't have any broken bones. There is quite a bit of swelling and edema in the soft tissue."

"Tell me something I don't know."

"I'm going to keep you overnight for observation."

JD's face crinkled. "I can observe myself just fine at home."

"Sorry. You took a pretty good knock to the noggin. CT shows no intracranial hemorrhaging, but I want to make sure swelling doesn't worsen."

"My shoulder hurts like hell," JD said, clutching at it.

"I would imagine so. You may have a torn rotator cuff. Follow-up with your orthopedist."

JD frowned at him.

"I'll have you admitted and transferred shortly. Try not to raise too much hell with the nurses."

JD smiled. "Who, me?"

Dr. Parker left, and I took a seat next to the bed.

"You talk to Scarlett?"

"Not yet." JD reached for his phone that sat on a tray table by the bed. "Look at this!" He displayed the shattered screen to me.

"I think the phone is the least of your worries."

"How's the car?"

"Fortunately, the car was outside the angle of the blast. It didn't get a scratch."

He breathed a sigh of relief.

Denise called. "I've got something to talk to you about, but first, is he okay?"

"Yeah, he's gonna make it." I filled her in on the details, then let her talk to Jack. They conversed for a few minutes, and he may have embellished a few details about the size of the blast and how far he flew through the air.

He handed the phone back to me, and Denise said, "I have a lead on the Santa Slayer."

35

"Sue Cassidy just called the station after hearing about the Taffy Beach murder on the news last night. She's convinced her coworker, Ryan Foster, is the slayer."

"Why is she convinced?" I asked.

"Apparently, Ryan made threats at work. He got fired recently and said *they all deserved to die a horrible death. And they'd be lucky if he didn't come back and torch the office*. Sue said she always got a creepy vibe from him. The recent firing could be a stressor that pushed him over the edge."

"Where does she work?"

"An internet security company," Denise said. "And guess what kind of car Ryan drives?"

"A black Mustang?"

"Midnight blue. And get this. Sue said he showed up to the company Christmas party drunk and wearing a Santa costume."

"Have you told Daniels about this?"

"Yep. Sue came down to the station and made a statement. Daniels is trying to get a warrant." She paused. "Ryan fits the description of our killer to a T. Sue said Ryan recently broke up with his girlfriend and took it pretty hard."

"Nice work."

"Thank you," she said with a smile in her voice. "I'll keep you posted."

Denise ended the call, and it wasn't long after when the nurse arrived to transfer JD to the trauma ward in the main hospital. The nurse rolled his bed through a maze of hallways, up the freight elevator, and onto the ward. Jack was given a private room.

A nurse recognized him. "Weren't you just in here with a gunshot wound?"

JD smiled. "Yes, ma'am."

"You must like it here."

"It has its own charm, but I'm really just thinking of creative ways to see you."

She chuckled. "Well, you know I'll take care of you."

"I know that you will."

JD grabbed the remote and turned on the TV. A replay of Paris Delaney's segment from the warehouse was on. There was a shot of the ambulance pulling away and a cut to the interview with the sheriff and me.

Denise called back. "Daniels got the warrant for Ryan Foster. He says get to the station and take the usual crew."

"I'll be right there," I said with a grin.

JD was a tiny bit upset that he wasn't going to partake in the raid. I asked him if he wanted me to bring him anything back to the hospital afterward.

"A phone charger, a little whiskey, and maybe a cheeseburger."

"No whiskey for you, sir," the nurse said, overhearing our conversation as she stepped back into the room.

JD frowned. "Don't listen to her."

"He better listen to me. What I say goes around here."

"You ain't the boss of me," JD said.

"I am while you're in here, Sugar."

JD smiled at her.

"That smile might work elsewhere, but it ain't cute enough to make me bend the rules."

JD's smile turned into a frown.

"Take good care of him," I said to the nurse.

"I will."

"You realize that somebody out there wants us both dead," JD said. "I don't think they're gonna stop with the pipe bomb at the warehouse. Keep your head on a swivel."

"Always. You want me to have Daniels send a guard to the hospital?"

"I don't need a babysitter."

"Hang on a minute," the nurse said. "Somebody tried to blow you two up?"

We both shrugged and nodded.

"You're not exactly making me feel great about working on this ward with him here."

She was half-serious.

"Don't worry. No assassination attempt against me has been successful yet," JD said.

"I'm more worried about the innocent bystanders," she joked.

She had a point. Somebody went through a lot of trouble to make that pipe bomb. They wanted us out of the way for a reason. I called Daniels and told him to send a deputy to the hospital to keep an eye on things.

I left the trauma ward and hustled across the parking lot to the Porsche. I drove to the marina at *Diver Down*, grabbed my tactical gear, and suited up before heading to the Sheriff's Department. I met up with Erickson, Faulkner, Mendoza, and Robinson.

With a warrant in hand, we drove to the *Palm Shores* apartments. It was an eight-unit French colonial on Flamingo Drive. It was painted pastel yellow with white trim and royal blue shutters. Steps led to a veranda, a switchback staircase led to a second-story terrace, and another staircase led to the attic apartments with dormer windows. Two large oaks sprouting out of the sidewalk gave it shade. The paint was faded and peeling, and the trim under the gutters was stained from the rain. The building was built in the 1920s, and it had seen better days.

The deputies parked at the curb and the street was shrouded with oaks. There wasn't much available parking. I had to park around the corner in a tow-away zone. Nobody would tow patrol cars, but I worried about the Porsche. JD would have my ass if I got it towed.

I hopped out of the car and fell in line with the deputies as we rushed down the sidewalk. We climbed the steps to the veranda and took the switchback staircase up to the second floor. Faulkner banged on the door to unit #5.

"Coconut County! We have a warrant for your arrest," he shouted.

Mendoza kept watch on the ground in case the perp tried to jump out a window and escape.

Ryan pulled open the door moments later, looking bewildered. His brow knitted together. "What are you arresting me for?"

"Oh, just a few murders," I said. "That's all."

His face twisted. "What!?"

I read him his rights. "You have the right to remain silent..."

He didn't put up a fight. We had him in cuffs in no time. Robinson kept Ryan on the porch as I stormed into the crappy little apartment, searching for a Santa suit and a flamethrower.

Dishes were piled at the sink. The TV was on, and the coffee table was littered with empty plates, beer bottles, and a half-eaten bag of potato chips. There was a small joint in the ashtray.

It didn't take long to find the Santa suit and the flamethrower in the bedroom closet. We bagged and tagged the evidence.

"What are you doing with my flamethrower?" Ryan asked as I emerged.

"The question is *what have you been doing with your flamethrower?*"

He stared at me, utterly confused. "I haven't touched that thing in months. I was thinking about selling it."

Robinson took the perp by the arm, marched him down the staircase, and stuffed him into the back of a patrol car.

I hustled around the corner with my fingers crossed.

The Porsche was right where I left it.

I hopped in and followed the deputies back to the station, where I filled out an after-action report in the conference room under the sickly fluorescent light.

Ryan was processed, printed, and put into an interrogation room. I figured JD would want to see this, so I FaceTimed him and set the phone on a stand on the table to capture the interview.

"You can't video me," Ryan said. "I don't give you my consent."

"Sorry. I *can* video you."

"You have no reason to arrest me."

"You drive a midnight blue Mustang."

"Is that illegal?"

I shook my head. "You have a flamethrower."

"That's not illegal either."

"And you have a Santa suit."

"I guess Christmas is illegal now, too," he snarked.

"No, but all three of those things together make you a person of interest in the Santa Slayings."

His face crinkled. "What!?"

"Where were you last night?"

He thought about it for a moment. "I don't have to answer any of your questions."

"That's true." The smartest thing to do was shut up. But it was my job to get people talking even when it was against their best interest. "Maybe this is all a big misunderstanding, and we can clear it up."

"You're damn right it's a misunderstanding."

"It's my understanding you recently got fired."

"So?"

"You said that your coworkers *deserved to die a horrible death. And they'd be lucky if you didn't come back and torch the office.*"

His eyes narrowed at me. "Who told you that?"

"Who told me that is irrelevant. I'm asking you if you said it?"

His face tensed. He contemplated his next words. "I don't know if I said that exactly. I may have said that and a few other things. But they're all assholes. They fucking fired me."

"Can't imagine why?"

He scowled at me. "They didn't deserve an employee like me."

He definitely had an over-inflated view of himself.

"You recently broke up with your girlfriend."

"What business is that of yours?"

"The Santa Slayer has been killing couples. Our behavioral sciences expert believes this could be due to a recent breakup fueling ongoing animosity toward the opposite sex. Negative thoughts on love and relationships." We didn't have a behavioral sciences expert, but I was quoting Denise.

His face twisted. "I don't have any ongoing animosity. I got a new girlfriend. Kali leaving me was the best thing that ever happened."

"Really? You're not still bitter."

"I told you, I've got a new girl, and she's awesome."

"Where are you working now?"

"I'm in between employment opportunities."

"So, where were you the night of the murders at Fort Dawson?"

"I was with my girlfriend."

"And last night?"

"My girlfriend again."

I was hesitant to believe him.

"And what is your supposed girlfriend's name?"

"Tammy."

"So if I call Tammy right now, she'll verify your whereabouts?"

He swallowed hard. "Sure."

"You seem a little nervous about that. Are you positive?"

"Call her and find out."

"What's her number?"

36

Ryan gave me Tammy Tidwell's number. I ended the FaceTime with JD and dialed.

It went straight to voicemail. I left a message along with my number.

"She's probably at work," Ryan said.

"Where does she work?"

"She's a barista at Key Bean."

I called the coffee shop and spoke with the manager. He said Tammy wasn't working. I ended the call and stared across the table at Ryan. "Looks like you're shit out of luck."

"I'm telling you, I'm not your guy. I didn't do anything!"

"You know, I hear that a lot."

He glared at me.

I left him to sweat in the interrogation room and stepped into the hallway. Daniels had been watching from the observation room. He greeted me in the hall.

"How solid are you on this guy?"

"Growing less so," I said. "He fits the profile. Has the same build. I mean, what are the odds we catch a guy who drives the same car and has the same flamethrower? But this guy's speech and demeanor are different from the scumbag I talked to on the phone. Ryan isn't as smart."

"Maybe the guy you talked to on the phone was yanking your chain."

"Possible."

"What do you want to do?"

"Wait and see what his *girlfriend* says," I said in a sardonic tone. "If he actually has a girlfriend."

My phone buzzed with a call from Isabella.

"Tell me you got something good," I said.

"Quite a few things, actually. A girl on the catering staff is a student at Vanden University."

"Nothing shocking there."

"I'm getting to the interesting part. Her name is Autumn Clark, and she might be working for the Ministry of State Security."

"Chinese intelligence."

"She did a year in Beijing as a foreign exchange student. She's espoused support for the regime on social media and has decried American imperialism."

"You think she was recruited?"

"I do. I've been looking at Paul Brown's bank transactions. He's been getting ACH transfers in the amount of $50,000 per month deposited into his account. Want to know who's putting it there?"

"Autumn Clark."

"Bingo," she said.

"Paul Brown was selling secrets to the Chinese?"

"Sure looks that way."

"But why kill him?"

"Maybe he threatened to blow the lid on the whole thing. Maybe he wanted more money. Maybe he wasn't providing enough value."

"All good reasons," I said.

"Where do I find this college student of ours?"

"She lives in the Wharton tower. And from what I can tell, she has been involved with at least two other professors and a state representative."

"This is quickly becoming a matter of national security," I said, half joking.

"You may be more right than you think."

"I'll pay Ms. Clark a visit."

"Let me know how it goes."

I thanked her for the info and ended the call, then gave Sheriff Daniels the scoop.

"And you think this college student could have poisoned Brown?"

"She had access. I'm thinking we might have spooked her when we showed up at the catering company today."

"Was she there?"

"I can't be certain."

"What about the pipe bomb?"

"No telling what kind of skills she might have if she was recruited and trained by a foreign intelligence agency. They sure were funding the operation well."

"I don't know how you get your information, and I don't really want to know. But I'm glad you get it." He gave me a pat on the back as he ambled down the hallway.

I left the station and drove to Vanden University. I parked in the lot near the Founders Court, then hustled across the quad, weaving through the grand Georgian buildings toward Wharton Tower.

College students slinging backpacks crisscrossed the campus, though it was pretty sparse. As soon as finals were over, students headed home for the holidays. There were a few students that lingered on campus, but Vanden mostly became a ghost town from mid-December until mid-January.

The Wharton Tower was a luxury high-rise for students with wealthy parents. The lobby had a lounge area, coffee shop, sandwich shop, and other amenities. I pushed inside and strolled to the elevator bank. During peak class time hours, it could take a while to move up and down the floors, but I caught a lift and rocketed up to the 16th floor in no time. I banged on the door to #1622, hoping to catch Autumn Clark.

A young girl's voice filtered through the door. "Who is it?"

I held my badge to the peephole. "Coconut County. I need a few words with you."

A beautiful blonde with hair that dangled just past her shoulders pulled open the door. She wore white jogging shorts, a pink sports bra, and white sneakers with pink socks. She was very well coordinated. She had piercing blue eyes and a deep tan.

This girl wasn't Autumn Clark. She looked nothing like the DMV photo that Denise had given me before I left the station.

"Is Autumn around?"

"She already left for holiday break. She in some kind of trouble?" the girl asked with her face scrunched up.

I shrugged. "I don't know. Maybe. When did she leave?"

"Maybe an hour ago. She was in a hurry. She packed her stuff quickly."

"You mind if I take a look around?"

She hesitated for a moment. "Uh, okay. Sure."

She stepped aside and motioned me into the dorm room. "I was just about to leave. Will this take long?"

"Only a minute."

It was a pretty standard room—two twin bunk beds, two desks, two dressers, and a window that looked out over campus. These units shared a common bathroom with their suite-mates, who had the opposite layout on the other side.

Thick college textbooks lined the bookshelves. A movie played on the flatscreen TV mounted on the wall. The walls were painted pink, and there were pictures of guys tacked up. Teen idols. Pretty standard dorm room stuff.

"How long have you two been roommates?"

"Just this semester."

"You get along?"

She held out her hand and teetered it back and forth, indicating she wasn't too enthused about the situation. "I'm getting another roommate next semester."

"Why didn't you two get along?"

"Autumn's too uptight. Everything is always serious with her. And, my God, she talks nonstop about politics, and I just don't care. I don't want to hear it. I'm here to get a degree and have fun and maybe find a husband."

"Is this Autumn's desk?" I asked, pointing.

"Yeah, how did you know?"

"Because yours has a picture of a guy who I assume is your boyfriend. You have a bunch of colorful pens and a coffee mug that reads *don't talk to me until this level*. Your desk has much more personality."

The blonde smiled and flirted, "He's not my boyfriend."

"What's your name?"

"Brandi."

I started rummaging through the drawers in Autumn's desk and quickly found what I was looking for. A few 9-volt transistor batteries that happened to be the same brand as the one used in the pipe bomb. There were wires, wire cutters, ball bearings, and smokeless gunpowder. In the bottom drawer, I found pipes and end caps. "Did you ever see your roommate making a bomb?"

Brandi's pretty blue eyes rounded. "What!?"

I snapped on a pair of nitrile gloves and pulled out a pipe from the drawer, waving it in the air.

The blonde seemed stunned. "No. I've never seen anything like that before. I mean, I don't go rooting through Autumn's stuff."

I moved to the closet. It was half empty. Just a few items left dangling on the rack.

"Looks like she took most of her wardrobe."

"Well, I'm moving in with a friend on another floor next semester. I think Autumn was planning on keeping this unit."

"I'm not sure she's coming back," I said.

"That's fine by me."

"I don't mean to hold you up, but I need to get a team of forensic investigators in here."

Her eyes rounded again. "Why?"

"Because I think your roommate made a bomb that almost killed my friend today."

37

Forensic investigators swarmed the tiny dorm room, collecting the bomb-making material. Sheriff Daniels put out a BOLO on Autumn Clark, but something told me we wouldn't find her. If she was working as a spy for the Chinese, they likely provided her with an escape route. That escape route could be one or two things. A fake passport and a trip out of the country or an assassin's bullet. Perhaps they'd use a more subtle method like poison.

Brandi told me, and Isabella confirmed, that Autumn's parents were no longer living. She had no siblings, nothing to tie her to American soil any longer.

We wrapped up at the dorm, and I left campus, mulling the scenario over in my mind. Autumn Clark had plenty of time to slip the poison in Paul Brown's drink. Maybe it wasn't working fast enough, and she got nervous. Bashed him over the head as he leaned against the gunwale and dumped the body overboard. Paul Brown was a big guy, and Autumn Clark was a petite brunette all of 5'3", 105 pounds. Hoisting his body over the gunwale would have been awkward, to say the least. But, I guess stranger things have been known to happen. People do seem to become capable of unusual bursts of strength in times of high adrenaline.

I called Alexandria West as I drove back to *Diver Down*. "I heard about the explosion. Is JD okay?"

"He's going to be fine."

"Thank God. Do you know who's responsible?"

I told her my suspicions about Paul Brown selling secrets to the Chinese and informed Alexandria of our college student.

She groaned. "Do you have any idea how much data Paul leaked?"

"Not at this time. But you know the drill. Expect that your entire operation is compromised. I would do a full sweep of all of your systems and make sure your computers haven't been infected with any type of virus or keylogger."

"I appreciate the heads up. This is state-of-the-art technology that will give American forces a competitive advantage on the battlefield." Her voice tightened. "That son-of-a-bitch. Not only is it possible our adversaries will have our latest technology, but it's also likely our designs will be knocked off and manufactured for less."

"You know knockoffs are never the same."

"So, is that it? Is that your case? Is it closed now?"

I suspected she was asking for personal reasons.

"It's not exactly closed. Our suspect is still at large, and we have no definitive evidence that Autumn Clark killed Paul

Brown. But I'm relatively certain that the forensics team will connect the pipe bomb to her."

"Be careful out there, Deputy. It would be a tragedy if you got yourself killed before this case is closed."

"Trust me, I'm not going anywhere."

I pulled into the parking lot at *Diver Down*. "Listen, I gotta run. We'll talk later."

"Indeed we will."

I hopped out of the Porsche, strolled into the restaurant, and took a seat at the bar. Harlan was at the end, sipping on a beer as usual.

"How's Jack?" Teagan asked.

"I'm sure he's driving the nurses crazy."

"I have no doubt. What can I get for you?"

I ordered grilled chicken and vegetables and a cheeseburger to-go for Jack. After I ate, I jogged to the *Avventura*, grabbed an extra phone charger and a change of clothes for JD. Then I hustled back to *Diver Down*, grabbed the to-go meal, and raced back to the hospital.

Jack was happy to get the burger. The hospital food was okay, but nothing to write home about. He chowed down, and I gave him the scoop on Autumn Clark.

My phone buzzed with an *unknown call*, and I knew it was trouble the minute I looked at the display. I swiped the screen, held the phone to my ear, and a familiar voice filled me with dread.

38

"Y ou guys aren't very good at your job, are you?"

"I beg to differ," I said.

"You've got the wrong guy in custody," the Santa Slayer said. "I mean, this is almost comical."

"I'm glad you find it amusing."

"It is highly entertaining watching you two bumble about. I heard about your partner. I hope he's okay."

"He'll be just fine. Thank you for your concern."

"Are you going to let that poor, innocent man go?"

"How do I know you're actually the killer?"

"I've already told you pertinent information that only the killer could know. What more do you want from me?"

"I want you to turn yourself in."

He chuckled.

"We both know that's not going to happen."

"I'm closing in. I know you drive a Mustang."

"You know that I drove away from the scene of the crime in a Mustang. You don't know if the Mustang belongs to me. It could have been stolen."

"There were no vehicles matching that description reported stolen."

"I could have returned the vehicle before anyone knew it was gone."

"You're getting careless."

"Video doorbells are everywhere. It was inevitable. Besides, you have surveillance footage from the first killing, and that didn't help you. I could pass by you on the street, and you would never know it's me. That's terrifying to you, isn't it?"

"What's terrifying to me is that you can murder people in cold blood for no reason."

"But murder with a reason is justifiable? I mean, I've done some digging on you, Deputy. It seems you have done your fair share of killing."

"All justifiable."

"All? Are you sure about that?"

I wasn't going to play this clown's game.

"I'll tell you what... Release the guy you've wrongfully imprisoned, and I won't kill anyone else tonight."

"Why do you care about the guy who's warming your seat in lockup?"

"I don't care about him. I just like making you jump through hoops."

"If you keep doing what you're doing, you're gonna get caught. Everybody slips up."

"It's so heartwarming to hear you look after my interests," he said, mocking me. "Gotta go. We'll talk soon."

I dialed the sheriff and updated him. He responded with a groan. "The DA likes the case against Ryan. Are you sure?"

"Positive. We've got the wrong guy."

He sighed. "I'll talk to the DA."

"The Slayer says he's going to kill again if Ryan isn't released."

The sheriff's voice tightened. "You find that scumbag," he said in a low growl. "I don't like ultimatums."

I hung out with JD at the hospital. With an insignificant amount of sleep the night before, I crashed out right there on the sleeper chair. I only meant to lean back and close my eyes for a minute.

A nurse came in around midnight to check on JD, and that stirred me from my slumber. I told Jack I'd catch up with him in the morning and headed back to the marina. He was groggy and doped up, so I doubted he would remember my leaving.

Autumn Clark was not coming to finish the job. She was probably long gone by now. Bomb-makers are cowards. It's a passive-aggressive way to kill someone. The bomb-maker isn't around to see the destruction and suffering first-hand. It allows them to compartmentalize. They can justify their actions with all kinds of lofty narratives supporting their cause. But they lack the stomach to do the real wet-work themselves.

Needless to say, I didn't hold Autumn Clark in high esteem.

Buddy greeted me excitedly when I returned to the *Avventura*. I took him out for a midnight stroll, then climbed into bed.

I slept solid. I don't think I moved until 9 AM when Denise called. I snatched the phone from the nightstand.

"The lab says the death threat the Christmas lights judges received was printed on an Eptex 3500 XT. No fingerprints. It was mailed from a dropbox on the corner of Silverado and Westwood Streets. Last pickup from that box is 5 PM."

The make and model sounded familiar. I searched my brain, and a memory flashed in my head. "I'll check out the mailbox and see if any nearby cameras captured footage. But I think I may know who sent that letter." I paused. "Please tell me no one else was torched last night by the Slayer."

"Ryan Foster was released, and the charges were dropped."

"Seems like our killer stuck to his word."

"Today's a new day. Maybe he just wasn't in the mood to kill anyone last night."

"Let's hope he stays in that mood."

I ended the call, dragged myself out of bed, and took a shower. After breakfast, I took Buddy for a walk, then hopped into the Porsche and drove to *Whispering Heights*. I parked the car across from Esther Murray's house. Her new lighting display was still in one piece.

Stephen Bradford had recently purchased that exact printer. The box was at the curb the day after the vandalism. I strolled the walkway and banged on his door. He answered a few moments later with a pleasant smile. "Deputy Wild, what can I do for you?"

I handed him a copy of the death threat. I wanted to see his reaction.

"What's this?"

"The letter all three judges received."

"Oh, right. I heard something about that. It's just terrible what people will do over something as silly as a Christmas light contest." He handed the copy back to me. "Why are you telling me about this?"

"It was printed on the Eptex 3500 XT."

He shrugged, unfazed. "So?"

"You own a printer like that."

"So do a lot of people. You know, that printer was rated #1 in its class by *Electronic Digest*."

"I haven't been following the trends lately."

"I bet there are dozens on the island. Hundreds, perhaps."

"So, you didn't write the letter, print it on your machine, and send it from the mailbox around the corner on Silverado?"

He smiled. "Nope. You got the wrong man. Judging by the news, that's happening a lot to you." He took a deep breath.

"I gotta say, I really am impressed at the lengths you're going through to solve this thing. It doesn't seem like it would be a priority."

"We take death threats seriously around here."

"Good to know."

There was a long, awkward pause.

"If that's all, I need to get back to my day."

"That's all for now," I said. "I'll be in touch."

Stephen forced another smile, then closed the door.

I needed something a little more conclusive if I was going to haul him down to the station.

I left *Whispering Heights*, drove to the corner of Silverado and Westwood, parked the car, and searched the area for security cameras.

I couldn't find any that had a direct angle on the mailbox.

Our Christmas light terrorist either got lucky or knew it was a safe mailbox to send threats from.

I got another anonymous call as I walked back to the Porsche. I wasn't too big on anonymous calls these days. I answered and held the phone to my ear. "This is Deputy Wild."

39

"I have information that's relevant to the Paul Brown case," the woman said. Her voice was distinctly different from the last woman who called me.

"What kind of information?" I asked.

"I know why he was killed."

"I know about the theft of company secrets."

She seemed befuddled. "No, that's not why Paul was killed."

"Are you trying to tell me Paul wasn't selling secrets to the Chinese government?"

She hesitated. "I don't know. He may have been, but there's something else."

"Like what?" I asked. My voice was loaded with frustration and doubt. I was sure she could pick up on it.

"If I tell you, are you going to pursue this? Or are you just going to dismiss it?"

"If it's something of merit, I will pursue it. I'm sorry if I'm a little doubtful, but the last anonymous caller tried to kill me."

"So you see how dangerous this is?"

"Let's get down to it."

"Paul Brown may have been selling secrets. That wouldn't surprise me. But he found out something about the AIBCIS, and they killed him for it. The same thing I found out."

"What did you find out?" I asked, growing weary of her game.

"That it doesn't work."

That hung there for a moment.

"What do you mean it doesn't work?"

"It's bullshit. It doesn't work. There's no AI system. It can't properly identify *friend* or *foe*. It can't assess threats. At least not to the level they claim it can. All the research, tests, and data are fraudulent. On top of that, these optics aren't even manufactured in the United States, as they claim. They're cheap scopes, imported and rebranded."

"You're telling me the United States government just paid $289 million for a battlefield information system that doesn't work?"

"That's exactly what I'm telling you."

"Can you prove any of this?"

"Yes, I can. I have the data on a thumb drive."

"Where are you calling me from?"

"This line is not secure. I'm not stupid. I'm calling you from a prepaid cellular at a location that can't be tracked to me."

"I'll need a copy of the data."

"We can meet, and I can hand you the drive. I want nothing to do with this. I'm putting my life in jeopardy by calling you."

"I take it you work for West-Tek?"

She said nothing.

"You wouldn't have been able to get the data otherwise." I paused. "Have you talked to Alexandria about this? How much does she know?"

"Are you kidding me? I haven't told anyone. How could Alexandria not know? If there's anyone who had an incentive to kill Paul Brown, it's her. Paul could have blown the lid off this whole thing. Knowing Paul, he probably tried to extort money from her."

"Doesn't sound like you have a high opinion of the guy."

"Not at all. He'd sell out his own mother for a buck."

I looked at my watch. "Meet me at the pier at Taffy Beach in half an hour."

"I don't want anyone seeing us together."

"Send me a download link."

"No. Everything on the internet leaves a trail. These people have ways of finding stuff out."

"Okay. I'll walk underneath the pier. You can drop the thumb drive down to me. Make it look casual."

She was silent for a moment. "Okay. I can do that."

"Are you willing to testify?"

"I don't think you're aware how deep this goes. How many people are involved. A lot of people make a lot of money off these types of deals. They don't like it when people mess up the gravy train. I've seen what happens. People die mysteriously. A car crash. A skiing accident. A sudden illness. They have a million ways to make people disappear."

"Who is *they*?"

"I don't know, and I don't want to know. But you know what I mean." She paused. "I'll see you in half an hour, Deputy."

The line went dead, and I slipped the phone into my pocket.

40

C renshaw was always eager to get out of the office and go on covert operations. I recruited him for the mission and swung by the station to pick him up. The kid was excited to ride in JD's new Porsche. Usually, we were in a cramped surveillance van.

Crenshaw brought a camera with a long telephoto lens. I wanted him to snap photos of our mystery woman for identification later.

"This is pretty badass," Crenshaw said, ogling the sports car.

I agreed.

"I'd pick a different color. Don't get me wrong, I'd take it."

"Everything with Jack has to be loud."

"This is certainly loud." A grin tugged his lips. "Get on it. Show me what she can do!"

I mashed the accelerator, and the engine howled. The acceleration pinned us both against the seats. The car launched forward at an almost uncontrollable pace.

It put a grin on both our faces.

I drove to Taffy Beach and cruised down Oyster Avenue, parking at the curb by the sidewalk. The pier was 40 yards ahead.

I told Crenshaw to get a clear shot of the woman. I waited for the traffic to pass, then pushed open the door and stepped out of the car.

"Hold up a second," Crenshaw said. "What if I need to move the car?"

"You won't need to move the car."

"You know, like in an emergency situation."

"Jack would kill me and you if anything happened to this car."

"Nothing is going to happen to the car. At least let me listen to the radio."

I frowned and reluctantly tossed him the keys.

I moved around the car and walked down the sidewalk to the access stairs that led down to the beach. I hit the white sand and started plodding toward the pier.

The sun beamed down, glistening the water. Small waves crashed against the shore, and there were a few surfers out there trying to catch the tiny swells. The waves weren't much, but better than nothing.

I looked up, scanning the pier for anyone that looked like they had something to share.

An old man fished. A few couples held hands and strolled the deck.

A woman walked midway down the pier. She glanced around nervously, then leaned against the rail. She wore a wide-brimmed straw hat with oversized sunglasses and a white sundress with a royal blue floral pattern.

This had to be my contact.

She finally saw me, and I gave a subtle nod. She reached into her purse and pulled out the thumb drive.

I was maybe 20 yards away from the pier when a man wearing a hat and mirrored shades marched toward her.

In the flash of a second, he stabbed her multiple times.

Quick punctures.

Crimson blood blossomed her sundress.

A look of terror twisted her face. Her knees went weak, and she collapsed onto the deck.

The man snatched the thumb drive from her palm and sprinted down the pier.

The crowd screeched with terror.

An older gentleman approached the woman and knelt beside her. "I'm a doctor. Call 911!" he shouted at the gawking crowd.

They were too dazed to do anything.

Mr. Stabby's heavy boots clanked against the wood as I raced up the beach toward the berm. I climbed to the sidewalk as the perp hopped into the passenger side of a black SUV.

Tires squealed, and the engine howled as it launched from the curb. It had paper plates, and there was no doubt in my mind they weren't legitimate.

Crenshaw had seen the whole thing go down and hopped behind the wheel. He started the car, dropped it into gear, and launched forward, pulling alongside me in the Porsche. There was no time to argue about who was driving.

I hopped into the passenger seat, and Crenshaw jammed his foot against the pedal. The tires barked, and the Porsche took off. The turbos spooled up, and we gained on the black SUV.

The vehicle banked a hard left, and tires squealed again.

We followed, and inertia thrust me against the seat bolster. I figured it was time to buckle up.

The big bulky SUV barreled down the avenue.

We were on its tail in no time.

Crenshaw was having the time of his life. He had a smile wider than the Grand Canyon.

I held on for dear life, clutching the *oh shit* handle. I had never ridden with Crenshaw before and had no estimation of his driving skills or lack thereof.

So far, he'd been handling the car well. But it was a lot of power and could easily get away from the inexperienced. The rear engine made the car handle differently than your average front-engine vehicle. It required counterintuitive sensibilities—brake before the corner, get on the gas midway, and stand on the gas pedal if the rear broke loose.

Of course, the car had all the modern idiot-proof traction control features. But this kind of driving was well past the idiot zone.

I called the Sheriff's Department and told them we were in pursuit of the black SUV. I gave them the plates and our current location and made sure EMTs were en route to the victim, though I didn't have high hopes. The damage inflicted was precise and lethal. This killer knew what he was doing.

41

The perps took a right at the next intersection, then a quick left, heading the wrong way down a one-way street. The top-heavy SUV rolled from side to side with each turn.

Crenshaw handled the S-curve with aplomb.

I cringed as we barreled down the narrow lane, passing the double red and white *Do Not Enter* signs. Cars were parked on inset shoulders on either side as we zipped through the residential segment.

My heart pounded, and my fist white-knuckled the door handle.

The SUV took a left on Tadpole Lane. It swept wide and took out a green trash bin and a blue recycling bin. Plastic water bottles and milk cartons launched into the air and bounced across the asphalt.

We barreled through the mess, plastic crunching under the fat tires.

The lane narrowed ahead. A lawn crew was parked on the shoulder with a trailer full of lawnmowers and leaf blowers.

It was a tight squeeze.

The SUV roared, and the Porsche howled.

Tall palms lined the roadway.

Crenshaw stayed right on their tail. They couldn't shake us.

The scumbags blew through the stop sign at the intersection ahead.

Tires screeched, and horns honked.

We followed just as the cross-traffic started moving again.

More honks.

The SUV veered into the oncoming lane, passing a gray minivan. The perps swerved back into their lane to avoid a car parked along the shoulder.

We got stuck behind the gray minivan for a moment, then Crenshaw swerved to pass them.

Ahead, an older woman backed out of her driveway without looking.

The SUV veered again, and tires squealed.

The woman finally stopped, and we barreled past her bumper and kept after the perps.

I hated chases through residential neighborhoods. I thought about telling Crenshaw to call it off. With any luck, Tango One would be in the air soon.

The SUV swung a hard right on Quail Dove Lane. It was a two-lane road with a double yellow line and plenty of parking on the shoulder.

We followed.

A moped ahead slowed things.

When the traffic cleared, the SUV swerved over the double yellows and zipped around the guy, almost clipping him. Mr. Moped pulled to the side and flipped the SUV off, then flipped us off as we passed.

I kept waiting for the sound of rotor blades, but I didn't hear any.

The perps laid on the horn at the intersection ahead and blasted through the red light.

More horns honked, and tires screeched.

Cross-traffic zigged and zagged to avoid collision.

Crenshaw slowed, then inched through the red light when it was clear. He floored it across the intersection, and the engine screamed.

"If anything happens to JD's car, he's going to kill you."

"Nothing is going to happen," Crenshaw assured, stomping on the gas again.

We caught up with perps as the road opened up for a long stretch. The speed limit was 35 mph, and we were doing 107 mph. We zipped past a row of restaurants and boutiques. Cars were parked all along the curb, as well as bikes and mopeds. Gusts of wind from the SUV knocked a few bikes over.

At the next intersection, the thugs took a sharp left, squealing around the corner. The ass-end of the SUV lost traction and fishtailed, almost taking out a cyclist near the laundromat.

We took the corner with ease and barreled down the lane after them.

There was a stop sign ahead, but the SUV had no intention of slowing down.

This time, their luck ran out.

They blew through the stop sign and got T-boned by a white Super Duty truck.

BAM!

Tires screeched.

Metal crumpled, and glass shattered.

The impact thundered, and airbags deployed.

It was like two tanks slamming into each other, and neither wanted to give. The Super Duty had pushed the black SUV sideways, leaving it at an unnatural angle on Lazy Oak Lane.

Steam billowed from the engine of the Super Duty.

Mr. Stabby flung open the door and launched out, taking off on foot.

Crenshaw stopped at the intersection, and I hopped out. "Stay here," I commanded as I chased after Mr. Stabby.

I gave a brief glance to the driver of the SUV. He wasn't in good shape. He lay slumped at the wheel, splattered with blood. Side impacts can be particularly nasty. The sheer force can snap spines.

42

M r. Stabby's boots smacked against the asphalt as he sprinted down Lazy Oak. He veered onto the sidewalk, streaking past residential homes. He took a left at the end of the block, angling around a bicycle shop on the corner with several American flags hanging from the balcony.

I followed him onto Jefferson Avenue, and we raced down the block past a liquor store, a seedy massage parlor, and a little fleabag motel.

My heart punched against my chest, and my legs drove me forward. Sweat misted my skin, and I heaved for breath.

The dirtbag was fast.

He veered left and darted into the open doors of Team Coconut Fitness

It was a stupid move.

I followed and cautiously entered the facility. My eyes took a second to adjust from the blinding light outside to the dim interior. Team Coconut Fitness was a Spartan sweatbox where hardcore crossfitters and powerlifters worked out. There were free weights, dumbbells, and machines. People jumped rope, did box jumps, and pushed heavy sleds.

There wasn't any air conditioning.

You didn't really need it in Coconut Key, and this place was all about getting your sweat on.

There were grunts and groans, and the place smelled like sweaty socks and muscle cream. Hardcore muscle heads pumped, and veins bulged. Super-toned fitness babes with washboard abs worked their glutes. Some of them had bigger biceps than I did.

Mr. Stabby sprinted toward the rear exit, bowling over patrons, knocking people off balance, and causing heavy weights to hit the floor with deafening clanks. There were plenty of glares and angry growls. Most of which got directed at me as I followed after him.

"What the fuck is your problem, man?"

I didn't plan on sticking around long enough to clarify the situation.

I pushed through the rear exit into the blinding light of the alleyway. I chased the scumbag as he ran past the dumpster and took a left on Pelican Place.

I rounded the corner after him, and he kept running down the lane until he darted across the next intersection and slipped into a four-story parking garage that was next to an office building.

I chased him into the garage and saw him disappear into the central staircase. I drew my weapon and held up at the entrance to the stairwell. I swung the barrel inside and cleared the corners, then advanced up the switchback staircase, keeping my weapon aimed up the flight of steps.

Stabby exited on the second floor.

I held up when I reached the second-floor landing and carefully swung my barrel around the corner, and swept the parking area.

Muzzle flash flickered, and a bullet snapped past my ear and smacked the concrete, sending chips of debris and a plume of dust into the air.

I ducked back into the stairwell, my heart pounding twice as fast as it was before.

I leaned against the concrete, then swung the barrel of my pistol around again, trying to get a shot at the perp. He had crouched low between cars, out of sight. The ramp sloped down, and the concrete walls were slotted, allowing a view of the neighboring ramp. *Visitor Parking* was stenciled on the walls. Green tinted fluorescents glowed overhead.

I advanced from the stairwell, keeping low to the ground, and huddled behind a parked car, using the wheel for cover. I looked underneath the car to see if I could catch a glimpse of the scumbag moving.

I saw nothing except spots of oil on the concrete.

Then I saw his boots as he sprinted toward the wall and slipped through a slot to the level below.

I darted back to the staircase, spiraled down, and exited the well, cautiously making my way around to the other side.

An older woman had pulled into the garage in a silver four-door.

Mr. Stabby blocked her path and aimed his pistol at her.

Terror filled her eyes.

He pulled her from the car, tossed her to the ground, and hopped behind the wheel. He dropped the car into gear, and his foot hit the gas. The tires squealed, echoing throughout the parking garage.

He barreled straight toward me.

I dove between two parked cars, tumbling to safety.

Tires squealed again as he rounded the corner and darted out the same way we had entered the garage.

I climbed to my feet and rushed to the old woman, who still lay on the ground. I displayed my badge as I knelt beside her. "Are you okay, ma'am?"

43

The lady was okay. A little traumatized and a few bruises, but she'd be just fine. I asked her if she wanted me to call an ambulance, but she declined. Daniels put out a BOLO on a silver Corolla, and I stayed with the woman until deputies arrived.

Crenshaw pulled the Porsche into the garage after I gave him my location.

"Out," I said.

"Let me drive back to the station," he said.

"You've done enough driving today."

"I did pretty good, didn't I?"

"You didn't wreck the car. So, yes, that's pretty good. Might as well quit while you're ahead."

He put the car in park and reluctantly hopped out. He circled around the passenger seat, and I climbed behind the wheel.

"That was just awesome." He couldn't stop grinning. "Totally awesome."

"I'm glad you're having fun," I said with a healthy dose of sarcasm.

"I gotta do more stuff like that."

"Well, when you have your own Porsche, you can go chase your own bad guys."

"You think I could become a deputy?"

I gave him a look like he was insane. He probably was. "The department needs you in IT."

"Yeah, yeah, I know. But this was too much fun."

"Wait till they shoot back at you. It's not quite as fun."

I drove out of the garage and headed back to the Sheriff's Office. When we pulled into the parking lot at the station, I said, "Not a word to Jack."

Crenshaw raised his hands innocently. "I'm not going to say anything."

"He'd have a fit if he knew what we were doing in his car."

"Mums the word. I swear. I don't want that guy pissed off at me. He's crazy." He thought about it for a second. "You're crazy too. But I'm not sure your friend is all there."

I stifled a chuckle.

We strolled into the office, and Crenshaw went back to his usual duties. I found the sheriff and brought him up to speed. We chatted in his private office. He sat behind his desk and looked at me with irritated eyes. "And can you corroborate anything this informant said to you?"

"Without the data she was going to give me, no. I can't."

"Well, it looks like she took her secrets to the grave."

I frowned. "Who was she?"

"Emma Fairchild. 27. Single mother. Worked for West-Tek."

I cringed. "What about her kid?"

"Department of Children and Families is handling that. My guess is they're going to track down the father, and he'll take custody."

"I think I need to have a talk with Alexandria."

"So you're on a first-name basis with a person of interest? Please tell me you're not banging her. That would look *really* good right about now." His eyes narrowed at me.

"I am not having any inappropriate relations with her. I have an inordinate amount of willpower."

Daniels rolled his eyes.

"But she does look pretty good naked."

Daniels glared at me.

"She's a bit of an exhibitionist. Just saying."

"I don't like this. I don't like it one bit. First, numb-nuts gets blown up, now you lose an informant. Any idea who these scumbags are?"

"You ID the driver of the SUV yet?"

"Working on it. He's dead."

"He didn't look too good last time I saw him."

"I suppose you have a theory about all this."

"We're talking military secrets, foreign intelligence agencies, and a government contract for a product that doesn't work. There could be any number of people involved. My guess is these hitmen were hired guns."

"Who hired them?" Daniels asked.

"If Paul Brown was about to blow the whistle, and Alexandria knew her product was defective, that gives her a hell of a motive."

"It does indeed."

44

"We need to have a little chat," I said when I called. I didn't play my cards just yet.

"I'm all for intellectually stimulating adult conversation," Alexandria said. "I'm about to call it quits for the day. How about we meet for drinks?"

I'd much rather interview a suspect in person. Body language is telling. "Where do you have in mind?"

"Red November. You know the place?"

"I do."

"See you there in half an hour, Deputy," she said with a voice full of optimism.

She was going to be in for a helluva disappointment.

I finished my report, then drove to Oyster Avenue. I managed to grab a spot at the curb. I put up the top for good measure. It was usually pretty safe on the street, but I didn't want to be responsible for JD's pride and joy.

I hopped out, clicked the alarm, and hustled down the sidewalk to *Red November*. I stepped inside, glanced around, and saw Alexandria at a high-top table near the bar. She waved when she saw me.

I moved to the table, and she greeted me with an enthusiastic smile. She already had a drink in her hand.

"What are you drinking? First round is on me."

"Whiskey," I said.

She flagged the waitress down. "Would you be a dear and bring my friend a glass of..."

"Jimmy Drake Black Label."

"A man with good taste."

"I'm a connoisseur of fine whiskeys," I said with a smile.

I didn't have any evidence. Unless she admitted something, I had nothing on her. Maybe something would slip out after a few drinks. If she had any involvement in Paul Brown's death or had hired assassins to take out the whistleblower, she'd surely have a tell. Even the best poker players have them.

"So what is it you're so desperate to talk to me about?" she asked. "Or are you still thinking about that black négligée of mine?"

"It was a nice négligée."

"It looks nicer when it's on the floor." She smiled.

"I have no doubt about that." I paused, surveying my surroundings, then refocused my gaze on her piercing blue eyes. "It's the AIBCIS system."

"Are you trying to pump me for information? You realize that is classified. I could tell you, but then I might have to—"

"Kill me? Somebody already tried."

Her eyes rounded, and her jaw dropped. "What!?"

"I keep getting these anonymous tips, but so far, they haven't exactly panned out as planned."

"Now I'm intrigued."

I told her about the informant's claims that the combat information system didn't work as advertised.

She looked like a deer in the headlights. She swallowed hard and shook her head. "No. That's not correct. That system works, and it's a good system. It will save American lives."

"Not according to this whistleblower."

"I've seen the test results. All the data. Does this whistleblower of yours have any proof, or is this a wild claim to smear my company?"

"Unfortunately, the whistleblower was killed, and I was unable to acquire the data."

Her eyes rounded even wider. "Killed?"

"Taken out by a team of assassins. Stabbed on the pier."

"I heard there was a woman that got stabbed on the pier, but they hadn't released any names yet. Do you know who?"

"Emma Fairchild?"

I watched Alexandria's eyes for her reaction.

"Oh my God. I just talked to Emma this morning. She said she was taking the day off to take her kid to a doctor's appointment." Alexandria paused. "This is all a little too much for me to process right now. Are you sure? Emma contacted you and said she had proof that the system was flawed?"

I nodded.

Alexandria shook her head again. "No. It just doesn't make any sense."

"You know what I think? I think Paul Brown was about to blow the whistle, and someone killed him before he had a chance. And I think that someone was you."

Her eyelashes fluttered. "What!? That's insane."

"You said you saw him in the companionway by the day head. You had a few words. Perhaps you pulled him into your stateroom. It's just a few steps away. You two were alone. He confronted you about the faulty equipment and demanded money to keep quiet. From what I know about Paul Brown and his willingness to engage in espionage, that doesn't seem terribly out of line."

Alexandria swallowed hard again. She was a woman who wasn't left speechless often, but it took her a second to choke out a reply. "That's utterly preposterous. Are you actually accusing me of what I think you're accusing me of?"

"Murder, fraud, attempted murder, a whole host of things," I said in a calm voice.

"I'm starting not to like you, Deputy Wild."

I shrugged. "Just doing my job."

"You're way off base. And you have no evidence to back up any of these claims. If you did, I suspect I would be surrounded by deputies and be in handcuffs by now."

I said nothing.

"You know, this has been a stimulating conversation, but not in the way that I had hoped. You'll forgive me if I decline to answer any further questions as it seems you're hellbent on pursuing the wrong avenue."

The waitress arrived and delivered my drink.

"Put both of these on Deputy Wild's tab."

"Certainly," the waitress said.

"Good evening, Deputy," Alexandria said as she pushed away from the table, fire in her eyes.

"The truth will come out," I shouted. "It always does."

Her high heels stabbed the floor as she stomped towards the exit.

She had a nice stomp. I'll give her that.

I finished my whiskey, paid the tab, then hit the restroom. The club was relatively new, and the bathroom wasn't a total disaster yet. It was a pretty standard layout—sink opposite the entry, a urinal to the left, and a private stall finished in gunmetal gray beyond that. The walls were matte black and the countertop red.

A drunk in a light gray suit stumbled in a moment after me and almost face-planted against the counter. He caught himself, stood up straight, and tried to compose himself.

I gave him a suspicious glance.

He proceeded to walk past me toward the private stall.

I was doing my business, but I could see the guy in the reflection of the chrome flush handle. He reached into his coat pocket for a pistol.

This was an awkward moment, to say the least.

45

I cut off the flow as best I could, but it was like a firehose at full pressure. I don't like people talking to me in the restroom, much less trying to kill me.

I spun around and grabbed the attacker's forearm before he could get the pistol aimed. I hammered a heavy fist into his rib cage a couple times and slammed his forearm against the stall partition until the gun dropped from his grasp and clattered against the tile. It slid into the stall near the toilet.

My shorts had slid down to my knees with the weight of my gun holstered in the waistband. It was an awkward way to fight.

His buddy guarding the bathroom outside must have heard the commotion. He rushed in and drew his weapon. With a big black pistol aimed at my face, the fight was over.

I raised my hands in surrender. I was pretty sure it was Mr. Stabby. He'd lost the ball cap and the mirrored shades, but it was him.

Gray Suit snatched my pistol from my shorts, then grabbed his from the tile.

"This is a little weird. Would you mind if I pull up my pants?"

He nodded.

I did and felt somewhat less vulnerable.

"We're all going to walk out of here together," Stabby said. "And you're going to pretend like everything is normal."

"I've got news for you. Nothing is normal around here."

"I'd cooperate if I were you, or people you love and care about are going to die."

I didn't like the sound of that. Was it a bluff? Or had they kidnapped someone I cared about?

I glared at him, then at Gray Suit.

"Let's move," Stabby commanded. "Don't make any trouble."

When I took a step forward, Gray Suit pistol-whipped me in the back of the head. Things got fuzzy after that, and I got an up-close and personal look at the tile.

That floor was pretty nasty.

I don't know how long I was out, but I woke up tied to a chair in a dim warehouse surrounded by rows of boxes and containers.

A blinding light on a stand shined on my face. It squinted my eyes, and I could barely make out the shape of several figures standing in front of me. My head throbbed and my neck ached. My wrists and ankles were bound to the chair by rope.

Mr. Stabby stepped into view. Gray Suit stood nearby. There was one, maybe two, figures in the shadows behind them.

"You're going to tell us everything that Emma Fairchild told you," Stabby said.

"She told me you guys were real pieces of shit," I said.

He cocked his fist back and smacked my cheek as hard as he could. His knuckles twisted my head to the side and sent a stabbing sensation down my jaw, through my spine. "I can see we're going to get along great. I'll ask you one more time to tell us everything Emma told you."

There was a part of me that wanted to give him a hard time. But there was also a part of me that didn't want another punch to the jaw.

That part won out.

"It's not much of a secret anymore," I said. "You guys are hustling bogus goods. Somebody's gonna figure it out, eventually. I just hope it's not the grunt in the field."

"Where's the data?"

My face crinkled. "You took the data drive when you stabbed Emma."

"Copies. Where are the other copies?"

"How should I know?"

That bought me another fist to the face.

SMACK!

The tinny metallic taste of blood filled my mouth. I spit a pinkish goo onto the concrete with a splat.

If Emma Fairchild was smart, she had made backups and stored them in multiple locations. An external hard drive. The cloud. Maybe she even sent a copy to an ambitious reporter. Or maybe she didn't do any of those things.

"The data. Who else has a copy of the data?"

"We can do this all night long, but the answer isn't going to change."

SMACK!

That got old quickly.

"I get it. You guys are the muscle behind this operation. But who's the brains?" I squinted my eyes, trying to look past the light at the figure loitering in the background.

He took a step forward and came into view, bow tie and all. "I'm the brains. But do I get credit for anything? No."

"Shut up, Preston," Mr. Stabby grumbled.

"What do you want credit for?" I asked the nerdy guy. "Pushing a crappy product?"

Preston's face reddened, and his veins pulsed. "I told them we needed more time. But they wouldn't listen. The project kept moving forward. I had to do something."

"So you manipulated the data."

"It would have destroyed the company if I didn't. Nobody cared. It just needed to look good on paper. Everybody wanted the deal to happen. Paul paraded me around at every sales meeting to sell the technical aspects. Then he had the nerve to threaten to expose the truth if he didn't get paid off."

My mind processed the info, and I picked up on something I should have noticed sooner. "You wanted to protect Alexandria."

"Of course."

It became clear to me he had a little crush on her.

"So, you killed Paul?"

"I didn't mean to. The bottle was in my hand. It was an involuntary response."

"You talk too much, Preston," Mr. Stabby said.

"Nobody asked you," Preston snapped. "Besides, you're going to take care of him, aren't you?"

"My job is to eliminate *all* threats," he said, glaring at Preston. It was a gaze that made the nerdy guy shrink.

"And who are you?" I asked Mr. Stabby.

His glare turned to me, and he answered with another fist to the jaw.

46

P reston wasn't running this circus. That much was certain.

"Tell me something. How did you get Paul overboard without anyone seeing?"

"Keep your mouth shut, Preston," Mr. Stabby said.

"You're not the boss of me. I'll say whatever I want."

"You're the one who created this situation."

"I didn't create the situation. I solved a problem. Paul was going to blow the whistle. He'd still be alive if he hadn't gotten greedy."

"Seems like you all have gotten greedy," I said.

Preston didn't like that. He growled, "Paul had no loyalty."

"But you do?"

"I've made so many sacrifices for this company. I'm not about to see it go down the tubes."

"You'll all be doing federal time."

He smirked. "No. We won't. Because we're cleaning up loose ends."

"Who's we?"

"I'm sorry, but this little Q&A session is over," Stabby said.

"You can grant a dying man a last wish, can't you? Satisfy my curiosity. How'd you get Paul overboard? You don't seem like you could lift a paper bag."

Preston's face reddened. "I got Paul over the gunwale all by myself, thank you very much! Granted, he fell against it after I hit him, so it didn't take much."

"And nobody saw you?"

His face froze. "Not really."

"Either somebody saw you, or they didn't."

"Shut up, Preston," Stabby barked.

"I'm tired of you telling me to shut up. I'm tired of being ignored. Everyone involved owes me."

"I've got news for you," I said. "Getting rid of me isn't going to solve your problems."

Stabby drew a pistol from his waistband and pressed it against my forehead. The cold steel indented my skin. The faint remnants of gunpowder filled my nostrils. "Are there any copies of the data?"

Torture a man long enough, and he'll say anything. I could take a lot of abuse, but I didn't have the answers they were looking for. So, I lied. "Emma sent a copy of the data to every major news outlet. The game is over."

"Bullshit."

"Whatever. Doesn't matter to me. You're going to kill me, right? What do I care about anything now?"

Stabby's finger tightened around the trigger.

"You're not going to do it here, are you?" Preston asked in a panicked voice.

"Why not?"

"Because it will make a mess."

"I don't work for you. I'm killing him here. You deal with it."

"Who do you work for?" I asked.

Stabby clenched his jaw. "None of your business."

"Preston's right. It's going to make a mess. Sure, you can mop it up and bleach it, but it's gonna look kinda funny when investigators Luminol the area. It will be the only spot in the warehouse that's been scrubbed. Unless you take the time to scrub the whole place, and who does that in a warehouse, anyway? Our forensics team is really good. And this is a West-Tek warehouse." I paused for dramatic effect. "I mean, you're a pro, right? This isn't your first rodeo. You're not this stupid, are you?"

His face reddened, and his eyes burned into me. He pressed the pistol against my head harder. He wanted to squeeze the trigger so bad his hand almost trembled.

Better judgment prevailed, and a moment later, he pulled the pistol away with a snarl.

"So, it does have a brain," I snarked.

He pistol-whipped me, clocking the grip against my temple. It opened up a gash, and warm blood streamed down my cheek.

It hurt like hell.

One of these days, I'd learn to keep my mouth shut.

"Call Jenson," Mr. Stabby said. "Tell him to get down here."

Preston looked terrified at the prospect. "I don't want to call him. He said to handle it."

"But you don't want me to handle it here. I'm not doing anything without authorization. Call Jenson. Tell him to come down here. Do not discuss anything on an open line."

Preston swallowed hard and dialed the phone.

47

"Hey, please tell this dickhead not to make a mess on company property," Preston said into the phone.

I heard a voice crackle through the speaker as he held the device to his ear. At this distance, it was barely audible. I couldn't make out what was said.

"Sure," Preston said after listening for a moment. He handed the phone to Stabby.

"Where do you want me to take care of this? ...I can do that."

The voice that I assumed belonged to Jenson said something else. "You got it."

He handed the device back to Preston, and Jenson barked a command.

"Yeah. Okay," Preston responded. "...Is that necessary? ... Okay. Whatever you say."

He ended the call, slipped the device into his pocket, and glared at Stabby. "I told you."

Stabby sneered at him, then told Gray to untie me. We were on the move.

Mr. Stabby kept his pistol aimed at me while Gray knelt down and untied my ankles. "Don't make any sudden movements, or I'll shoot you right here. I don't care what anybody says."

"You'll get nothing but cooperation from me," I said with a smile.

Gray made short work of my ankles and moved to my right wrist. The tight ropes left grooves in my skin and damn near cut off the circulation. With that free, Gray moved around the chair to my left.

Stabby took a cautious step back.

This was my moment and probably the only chance I'd get.

When the rope fell from my wrist, I grabbed Gray's tie and yanked him in front of me while snatching his pistol from his holster.

Muzzle flash flickered from Stabby's barrel as he fired two shots at me, which hit Gray in the back. He groaned and coughed blood. Fortunately, the bullets didn't exit his chest and hit me.

I squeezed the trigger, firing two shots through Gray's coat, drilling into Stabby.

Geysers of crimson blood erupted from his chest, and he fell back against the concrete, gasping for air. His lungs gurgled as he writhed and moaned.

His weapon clattered away.

With wide eyes, Preston turned tail and ran for the exit. His shoes clapped against the concrete.

I launched from my chair, sprinted past the blinding spotlight, and finally got a better look at the warehouse. I had no doubt that the crates housed thousands of poorly designed optics that would be sold to the US military.

I chased after Preston as he bolted through the main door and onto the loading dock. He jumped down to the asphalt as I exited the building, then sprinted to his black BMW. He clicked the key fob, and the lights flashed.

"You're not getting away," I shouted.

Preston hopped into the car, cranked up the engine, and threw it into reverse. The BMW launched away from the loading dock. Preston jammed the brakes, and tires squealed. He shifted into drive and punched it.

The tires spun as I dropped down to the asphalt and blocked his path, aiming my pistol at him.

The Beemer barreled toward me, the high beams on, slashing the hazy air.

He intended to run me over.

I'd call that assault with a deadly weapon. I'd be reasonably justified in using lethal force to bring the perp down, but I dove out of the way, tumbling to safety as he roared past me.

I needed Preston alive. I was pretty sure he'd rat everyone else out if under pressure.

In his zeal to take me out, he swerved too far and clipped the dumpster. The clatter filled the night air. Metal twisted. The impact folded the hood and right quarter panel. Radiator fluid hit the asphalt, and the smell of the hot engine filled my nostrils.

I sprang to my feet as Preston threw the car into reverse and backed away from the dumpster. Steam billowed from under the hood. He dropped the car into gear as I shot a rear tire out.

The bang was deafening.

He punched the accelerator, and the engine groaned. The tires squealed and gravel flew. The rim slipped inside the deflated tire. The car made it almost to the exit when the engine seized. The car stopped dead in its tracks.

The driver's door flung open, and Preston bolted out, giving me a terrified glance before sprinting away.

I gave chase and wasn't far behind.

Preston sprinted down the block. He wasn't in any kind of shape for a long-distance haul—and wearing loafers wasn't the ideal shoe for a foot chase.

I caught up to the wormy little bastard in no time and tackled him to the concrete.

He groaned as the breath escaped his lungs as he crunched under my weight. I wrenched his arm behind his back and slapped the cuffs around his wrists as hard as I could, the cold steel clanking against his wrist bones.

Once he was secure, I yanked him to his feet and hauled him back toward the warehouse. "You have the right to remain silent..."

"What are you arresting me for? I didn't do anything?"

I laughed. "You confessed to a murder. You were involved in the kidnapping of a law enforcement officer. You defrauded the US government. Do you want me to keep going?"

I called Daniels and told him to send a patrol unit, the medical examiner, and the forensic team.

The area swarmed with first responders in no time. Red and blue lights painted the warehouse, and investigators snooped around. Brenda and her crew examined Stabby and Gray. She used a mobile reader to take their fingerprints, and I snapped photos of the scumbags and sent them to Isabella for identification.

Preston was stuffed into the back of the patrol car and taken to the station, where he was processed and printed.

An EMT treated the gash on the back of my head and bruises and lacerations from the pistol-whipping. They recommended I go to the ER, but that was not on the agenda for the evening.

I filled out a report at the station, then paid a visit to Preston in the interrogation room.

The guy wasn't suited for captivity.

Sweat misted his skin, and he fidgeted nervously. He had a sickly pallor about him, and he looked like he was moments away from emptying the contents of his stomach.

I sat across the table from him, staring for a long time before I said anything. The silence was maddening.

Finally, he said, "So, what now?"

"You cooperate, give me the names of everyone involved, and turn over all the data. That's what. And if you're lucky, maybe you won't spend the rest of your life in jail."

48

Preston fidgeted, his eyes darting about, the wheels turning. Finally, he said, "I want a lawyer."

I tried to hide my displeasure. That was the end of the conversation. Once he asked, the interrogation was over.

"Normally, I'd say that was a smart move," I said, pushing away from the table. I stood up and stepped toward the door. "But a lawyer won't be able to save your ass. Have a nice life."

I knocked on the door, and a guard buzzed me out.

We put him in a holding cell packed with other new inmates. It only took about 45 minutes for him to change his mind. He was back in the interrogation room and ready to talk. "What kind of deal can you offer me?"

"Depends on what you have to offer," I said.

"I can give you the data and tell you the names of everyone involved. But I don't want to do any time."

I tried not to laugh. "You killed a man, Preston. You're going to do time. Right now, you're negotiating how long and where."

He swallowed hard. "I don't want to die in prison."

"Then start talking."

He was silent for a moment.

"Is Alexandria involved?"

He shook his head.

I lifted an incredulous brow. "You expect me to believe the head of the company didn't know the product didn't work?"

"Alexandria is the face of the company. She wines and dines and schmoozes. Jenson handles the finances and product development. Paul was trying to extort money. I overheard him when he approached Jenson."

"Jenson knew all along," I said.

Preston nodded.

I guessed, "He saw you kill Paul."

Preston nodded again. "It took care of our problem."

"So you, Jenson, and Paul were the only people who knew the product was defective until Emma found out?"

"I think."

"And Jenson hired the hitmen?"

"I don't know exactly where they came from, and I didn't ask questions."

"Who else is involved?"

"That's it. I swear!"

My eyes narrowed at him. He was holding something back. His nervous fidgeting gave it away. "You and I both know there's something more to it. What about the Colonel or the Deputy Director?"

He shook his head. "I don't know."

Either he didn't know, or he was afraid to say.

"If you're holding out on me..."

"I swear, I'm telling you everything I know."

I tried to pry it out of him, but he clammed up.

He made a sworn affidavit, and that was enough to get an arrest warrant for Jenson.

We stormed his home in Stingray Bay. His wife answered the door, shocked to see a tactical team that included Erickson, Faulkner, and Mendoza.

"What's this about?" Mrs. Ward asked.

"Your husband is under arrest for accessory to murder, among other things," I said.

She gasped as the team marched in.

We found Jenson in the living room, watching a large flatscreen. A bewildered look twisted his face as deputies surrounded him.

"This is a mistake," Mrs. Ward said, following us into the room. "My husband wouldn't kill anyone."

Jenson stood up and remained calm. "Anna, don't say a word to these people."

She stared deep into his eyes, trying to see if there was any truth to the allegations.

"Call Mike Landis. Tell him what happened." Jenson didn't put up a fight.

He kept his mouth shut as Faulkner slapped the cuffs around his wrists and marched him out. Faulkner read him his rights, but Jenson had no intention of talking.

I felt bad for the kids, watching their dad get carted away. He'd be going away for a long time.

We searched the house and confiscated Jenson's computer, laptop, and external hard drives.

At the station, he was processed and printed.

"I want to speak with my attorney," was the only thing he said in the interrogation room.

"You're going to need a good one," I said.

I pushed away from the table, banged on the door, and a guard buzzed me out.

Daniels greeted me in the hallway. "Got an ID on the getaway driver that was killed during the chase after Emma Fairchild's murder. Name's Brian Jacobson. I've been around long enough to sniff out phony backgrounds, and something stinks about this one. The guy's clean. Too clean. No prior criminal record. No record of military service. Nothing. It wasn't long after that I got a call from the FBI inquiring about him."

"His name was on a list," I said. "Somebody got an alert when you ran the background check."

"You know what that means better than I do. But I have my suspicions."

"That means he has friends in high places. Somebody provided him with a clean identity."

"Something tells me we're going to find the same thing with the two perps you killed at the warehouse. That reminds me, you're officially on administrative leave pending an investigation. Surrender your duty weapon. You know the drill."

I handed him my pistol.

"You can pick this up in the morning."

It was merely a formality at this point. But I was in no mood to kill anybody else in the few hours that remained in the day.

It was late, and I was tired, sore, and my head throbbed. Every time I moved my neck, I was reminded of Stabby's fist. I caught a glimpse of myself in the mirror in the bathroom at the station. It wasn't a pretty sight. Fat swollen lip, split in multiple places. Puffy eyes with dark circles and purple bruising. I looked like a boxer that had gone 12 rounds with a heavyweight champ. Maybe I *should* have gone to the ER for an evaluation.

I just wanted to go home, crawl in bed, and forget about West-Tek and Paul Brown.

I filled out an after-action report and contacted the Department of Defense's Criminal Investigative Service (DCIS), along with NCIS. The procurement fraud was their turf, and I was happy to let them take the lead on that. The feds planned to execute an early morning search on the West-Tek office. I'd let the federal investigators do the nitty-gritty of sifting through every email exchange and text message to find the co-conspirators.

My focus was the murder charge.

I called JD. They still hadn't released him from the hospital.

"Where the hell have you been? I've been calling you all afternoon."

"Long story." I caught him up to speed.

"No shit? All that went down today? Parker was supposed to cut me loose, but they're keeping me for another day for who knows what reason."

"You need anything?"

"A couple hot brunettes would do."

"I'm sure if you dig deep in that contact list of yours, you can find someone to entertain you. What happened to Juliana Morgan?"

"You know, things heated up, then fizzled."

"You seemed into her."

"Sweet girl. But she works too much. Plus, I didn't want to rush into anything too soon. I think she was looking for something more serious."

JD was notorious for rushing into things too soon.

"I feel bad," JD said. "All that went down, and I wasn't there to back you up."

"Well, next time, don't get blown up."

"I think that bomb was meant for you, not me," he said facetiously.

"I think it was meant for both of us."

I told JD I'd catch up with him in the morning, then caught a cab to *Red November* and picked up the Porsche. I drove back to the *Avventura* and climbed into bed with an ice pack. Isabella called as I was nodding off. "Got an ID on your perps."

That perked me up.

49

I sabella told me the same thing that Daniels did. Mr. Stabby and Gray Suit had fake backgrounds. "This goes pretty high up the food chain. Watch yourself."

"It's not my show anymore. DCIS is handling it."

"Just stay frosty," she said before ending the call.

It didn't take long to pass out after I talked with Isabella, but I didn't get much sleep. Daniels called in the wee hours of the morning. The phone buzzed incessantly on the nightstand for a few moments before I snatched it up.

"You're not gonna believe this. Or maybe you will."

"What happened now?" I groaned.

"Somebody torched the West Tek office. Arson investigators are there now. I'm sure it's just a random coincidence only hours before a federal raid," Daniels said with a healthy dose of sarcasm.

"You want me to get down there?"

"No point. The feds are all over it. ATF, DCIS, NCIS. They're coordinating with our department, of course."

"So why did you call me at 4 AM?" I said, trying not to sound too annoyed.

"Because we've got another problem. It seems that Mr. Murray decided to take justice into his own hands."

I groaned with anticipation.

"Apparently, someone decided to drive a truck through Esther Murray's decorations again, but her husband was waiting with a shotgun. Chaos ensued. I figure you might want to come down to the station and talk to him. He's in custody now."

"But I'm on administrative leave," I said, not wanting to crawl out of bed.

"You're reinstated. I conducted a thorough investigation and found you acted within protocol."

"Thanks," I said in monotone.

I ended the call and pulled myself out of bed. I took a shower, got dressed, and hustled down the dock to the Porsche. The car was growing on me.

I cruised down to the station, chatted with Daniels for a moment, then visited with Ben Murray in the interrogation room.

He sat at the table with a red face and a tight jaw. He recognized me when I walked in, and he unleashed a tirade. "This is absolute bullshit. These punks vandalized my home. I exercised my God-given right to defend my property, and I'm the one that gets arrested and put in jail? You people need to reevaluate your priorities."

"Our priority is a safe community. Discharging a firearm within city limits is not exactly responsible behavior."

"I can't defend my property?"

"The law says that you can use deadly force inside the home to protect your person from imminent danger. It doesn't say you can shoot at people who drive through your lawn. A stray bullet could injure your neighbor or damage property."

His face twisted into a scowl. He shook it off dismissively. "Nonsense. I used birdshot. That ain't going to go through a neighbor's wall across the street."

"From what I understand, you blew out the tire on the truck, and it hit another vehicle parked on the street, causing damage."

"Now that son-of-a-bitch will think twice before coming back to my house, I'll tell you that," Ben said. "Which is a hell of a lot more than your investigation has done."

"You described the truck to the sheriff as a maroon import. License plate XJC..."

"That's all I can remember."

"If you saw the perpetrators, do you think you could identify them?"

"The passenger, maybe. I didn't get a good look at the driver. But I tell you, that kid's face sure had a look of surprise when I took aim."

"You could have killed somebody, Ben."

"Well, that might put an end to the vandalism."

"And that could potentially put you behind bars for a long time."

"I ain't got that long left, son. Life behind bars ain't much of a deterrent at my age. Whose side are you on, anyway?"

"I'm on the side of justice. And I want to see justice done in this situation. I will do my best to apprehend these vandals. But I need you to let me do my job."

"So, what's the deal? Are there charges pending?"

"At the moment. You'll go before a judge and be arraigned in the morning."

Ben shook his head. "The system is broken. That's what it is. You punish victims, and you let these criminals walk. But hey, I guess now that I'm a criminal, maybe I'll get preferential treatment."

Ben would be put in a unit for the over-50 crowd. It was much calmer, with less violence than the regular unit. He wouldn't have a comfortable night, but he'd most likely be out in the morning unless the DA really wanted to hassle him with a charge of attempted murder.

It was out of my hands.

Ben grumbled as I left the interrogation room. "I'm a taxpayer. I vote!"

50

I made my way to the main office and took a seat at Denise's desk. She wasn't in yet. I used her computer to search the DMV records for a maroon truck that contained the letters XJC. It wasn't hard to find. The vehicle was listed to Bill Mason—mid 50s, lived in Whispering Heights a few blocks over from Esther Murray on Limpkin Street.

I drove the Porsche to Whispering Heights and banged on Bill's door. The night sky was just giving way to dawn. He lived in a mint-green two-story with mahogany doors, forest green shutters, a red-brick driveway on the side of the house, and a small lawn with a few shrubs.

Judging by his tone, he wasn't too pleased to be awoken at this hour. Bill shouted through the door. "Who the hell are you, and what do you want?"

"Coconut County. I need to talk to you."

He unlatched the deadbolt and pulled open the door with a scowl on his face. Bill was a simple-looking guy with short brown hair that was fading quickly to gray. His mustache was speckled, and his cheeks were rosy red. Other than that, his skin was a little pale, and he had a slight double chin. He was 6'1" and had a bit of a belly.

"You own a maroon truck?" I read off the license plate number.

"Yeah, why?"

"Can you tell me where you were between 3 and 4 AM last night?"

"I was in bed, where I'd still be if you weren't at my door."

He didn't much strike me as the type to go barreling through Esther Murray's yard, but you never know.

"Do you know Esther Murray?"

"Yeah. The woman with the lights. Everybody knows Esther."

"I see you went all out this year," I said, nodding to his meager lights. There were a few decorations up, but it wasn't anything special.

He looked at me flatly.

"Where's your truck now?"

"It's in the driveway. Why?"

I shook my head. "No, it's not."

His brow lifted with surprise. He stepped outside, trotted across the veranda and down the steps, then made his way around to the driveway. "Son-of-a-bitch!"

His hands tightened into fists, and he grew angrier than before.

"You got kids?" I asked.

"One. And that is more than enough." He stomped back up to the veranda and shouted inside. "Jeffrey! Get your ass down here. Now!"

Bill stepped into the foyer and shouted up the staircase again.

There was no response.

"Excuse me for a moment," Bill said to me before marching up the stairs.

His heavy footsteps rumbled the house and vibrated the veranda. I heard him push into an upstairs bedroom. There was a commotion, a little back and forth between him and his son, and a moment later, he marched Jeffrey down the steps to speak with me.

Jeffrey was about 17, sandy brown hair, brown eyes, and a slender frame. He was just a baby-faced kid, but there was mischief in those eyes. He looked me up and down. "Who are you?"

I flashed my badge.

The kid's eyes filled with terror.

"Where's my truck?" Bill asked his son.

The kid shrugged. "I don't know."

"You take it out last night?"

"No."

"Well, it's not here now," Bill said.

"Maybe it was stolen," Jeffrey replied.

"It was used in the commission of a crime last night," I said. "The vehicle was shot at by a homeowner, then subsequently crashed into a Lexus causing property damage."

Bill's face reddened, and he looked like he was about to pop. "So help me God, Jeffrey. If you had any involvement in this, I'll tan your hide."

"I didn't do anything. I swear."

"We're going to get to the bottom of this," Bill said. "That's for sure." He looked at me. "Excuse me for another moment." Then he glared at his son. "You stay right here."

Bill marched down the foyer and slipped into the kitchen.

"Where were you between 3 and 4 AM last night?" I asked the kid.

He stammered, "I was here. Sleeping."

It was bullshit.

"Kid, look at me. Do I look like I'm in the mood to be lied to?" I'd been through the wringer.

He shook his head.

"Start talking."

"I don't know anything."

My swollen, bruised eyes narrowed at him.

"What happened to your face?"

"I killed a couple guys last night that messed with me."

Jeffrey's eyes rounded.

His dad reappeared and stepped back into the foyer. He glared at his son again. "You know what I find really odd?"

Jeffrey shrugged.

"The spare key to my truck is missing."

"Don't look at me. Maybe you misplaced it."

That was not the thing to say to Bill at this particular moment. "I'm gonna put my foot in your ass if you don't stop this nonsense. Did you take my truck out last night?"

"No. I swear."

My phone buzzed with a call from Sheriff Daniels. "A patrol unit found the truck, or what's left of it."

"Where?"

"In an alley behind the Mega Mart. Somebody torched the vehicle."

"I'm talking to the owner," I said. "He claims the truck was stolen."

"That's interesting because the steering column was intact, and it didn't look like it had been hot-wired."

"I'm pretty sure I know what happened." I told the sheriff I'd speak with him later. I ended the call and slipped the phone into my pocket. "Deputies found your truck."

A look of relief and concern washed over Bill's face. That faded to pure rage when I told him the car had been set ablaze. He towered over his son, and his eyes were like lasers. He snarled, "Empty your pockets."

"What?"

"Turn them out!" Bill demanded.

The kid reluctantly did. As soon as he reached his hand into his pocket, an "oh shit" look twisted his face. Lo-and-behold, when the pocket liners came out, so did the spare key to the truck.

"What's that doing in your pocket?" Bill asked.

"I don't know how it got there."

"It's time to come clean," I said. "Right now, you're looking at criminal mischief, which is a third-degree felony punishable by a fine of up to $5,000 and or imprisonment of up to five years. Plus grand theft auto, if your dad wants to press charges."

The kid's jaw dropped, and his eyes widened.

51

"I've got an eyewitness that says there were two of you in the truck," I said.

Jeffrey shifted uncomfortably.

His father seethed.

"It wasn't my idea," the kid blurted.

"I'm listening."

He paused for a long moment, exchanged a glance with his dad, and shrank under the ire of his gaze.

"We were paid to do it."

"Do what?" Bill asked.

"Trash Mrs. Murray's yard."

I lifted a curious brow. "Who paid you?"

Jeffrey shifted again and fidgeted nervously. "Richard's girlfriend's mom."

"So Richard was with you?"

Jeffrey nodded. "It was his idea to torch the truck and say it was stolen. I didn't have anything to do with that."

Bill was about to have an aneurysm. The veins in his temples pulsed. He sucked in a deep breath and held it, trying not to explode. His body shook.

"Who's Richard's girlfriend's mother?" I asked.

Jeffrey stammered, "Paige Anderson."

"We need to go down to the station now," I said. "You're going to make a formal statement, and if what you say pans out, I'm sure the DA will be able to work out a lesser sentence."

The kid nodded.

We went down to the station, and Jeffrey was processed and printed. At 17 years old, the DA could *direct file* and charge him as an adult. He was put into an interrogation room where he confessed again and made a sworn affidavit implicating his friend Richard Starnes and Paige Anderson.

I was able to get warrants, and I went with Mendoza to make the arrests.

Paige denied any involvement at first, but a search of her home turned up the same model printer used to make the death threats.

Tears streamed down Paige's cheeks as she was stuffed into the back of the patrol car. On the drive back, it all spilled out. "I just wanted my mother to win once. I don't know how many years she has left."

She tried to make herself out to be the victim. She could try all she wanted, but it wasn't going to fly.

"You caused a lot of property damage," I said. "Two kids have screwed up their lives because of you. And you almost got somebody killed."

Paige sobbed even more.

She was booked at the station.

Erickson and Faulkner picked up Richard Starnes. He ratted out Paige as well.

I assured the judges of the competition there was no longer any danger, and they should go about their judging without fear. After all that had gone on, I was anxious to see who would actually win this year. Esther only had a few days to revamp her display once again.

After I wrapped up at the station, I headed to the hospital to check on JD. He had sent me a text that he was due to be discharged. I'd been keeping in touch with him all morning.

I brought him something from *Juicy Burger,* and he was most appreciative. But he still managed to gripe. "I can't believe I got stuck in here while you wrapped up the cases. Save a little fun for me, why don't you?"

"Trust me, there's plenty of fun left. There's still a killer in a red suit running around."

"Well, he hasn't killed anybody in a couple days. Maybe he's gone on hiatus."

We chowed down, and I waited around for his discharge paperwork to come through. Finally, the nurse came in with a wheelchair to escort him down to the passenger pickup and drop-off point. It was hospital policy. They didn't want to be responsible for falls.

I brought the Porsche around, and JD climbed from the wheelchair and hobbled to the car. He carefully inspected it for damages before easing himself into the passenger seat. He was still sore as hell. He waved goodbye to the nurse, then asked, "Any trouble with the car?"

"None at all," I said with a straight face.

"No accidents? No vandalism?"

"I've been driving it like a grandma." I smiled. It wasn't a lie.

He gave me a suspicious glance as we pulled away. I took him to the house. He showered and changed, then we headed by the rehab facility to see Scarlett.

What had started as a few obsessed fans had become several dozen. They loitered outside, hoping to catch a glimpse of the star.

The minute Jack stepped out of the car, a fan shouted, "That's him!" He pointed a finger, and the crowd swarmed JD.

We braced for the horde.

"Do you think you could get us autographs?"

"I'll see what I can do," JD said.

It was the same guy that had gotten an autograph the other day.

Jack gave him a suspicious glance.

The rambunctious crowd closed in. Somebody bumped into somebody else, and that somebody bumped into Jack.

He groaned with pain, still sore.

"Enough!" I shouted, stepping in between him and the mob, acting as his personal bodyguard. "Make room. Now!"

The crowd took a step back, but still smothered us.

I led the way and ushered JD into the facility. The security guard stood at the door. He just shook his head. "Been like this all day, every day, since she's been here. Never seen anything like it. Every day there are more. I'm about to call Coconut County and have them run off for trespassing."

I don't think he realized we were cops.

"It is private property, after all," I said.

We checked in at the reception desk, and the receptionist let Scarlett know we arrived. We caught up with her in the lounge and she gave Jack a big hug which made him wince.

"Easy there!"

"Sorry, excuse me for caring," she said.

"You can care. Just don't squeeze so hard."

"You look pretty good for someone who got blown up. I'm glad you're okay." Scarlett shifted her gaze to me. "You, on the other hand, I can't even go there. What happened to you?"

"You should see the other guy."

"Something tells me the other guy's dead."

I nodded.

"I go into rehab for a couple weeks, and all hell breaks loose."

JD scoffed. "I think all the chaos followed you here. Nothing like this ever happened in Coconut Key before."

She rolled her eyes. "Sell that to someone who doesn't know any better." She paused. "Why are you still doing this? Shouldn't you be relaxing and enjoying your golden years?"

Jack's face tightened. "I'm not in my golden years yet."

"I just worry about you guys, that's all."

JD scoffed. "*You*, worry about *us*?"

"What!? I do."

"You've been causing me worry your whole life. Now you know what it feels like."

She rolled her eyes and changed the subject. "You know what I'm craving?"

"Besides a little freedom?"

"That would be nice." Scarlett was more than ready to get out. "Could you guys bring me back a Lobster Grilled Cheese roll from Lobster Lucy with bacon and jalapeño?"

"You know the rules," JD said. "No outside food or beverage."

She pouted. "Rules are meant to be broken."

"You're in here because you broke a few rules."

"We're not going there."

"But you know, Lobster Lucy does sound good. We should catch the Holiday parade too. I'll be more than happy to text pictures of our meal."

She gave him a playful scowl. "Text away. I don't have access to my phone, which is the worst part of this."

"A little digital detox is good for the soul. Clears the mind."

She laughed. "What do you know about a clear mind?"

Now it was Jack's turn to make a face at her.

After our visit, Scarlett signed a few autographs for her adoring fans. The crowd mostly dissipated except for a few diehards. We hopped into the Porsche, and I drove to the historic boardwalk. We found a place to park not too far away, then strolled the boardwalk as the sun set on the horizon, painting the sky in pastel colors of orange and pink. Boats swayed in their slips in the marina. A hostess seated us at the patio table overlooking the water. It wasn't a bad spot to catch the sunset.

Lobster Lucy boasted *the best tail in Coconut Key* on their sign. A painting of a buxom pinup girl with a lobster tail showed off her backside. She looked more like a mermaid. A mer-lobster, with claws.

Lucy owned the joint, and she'd been serving all varieties of lobster rolls since the late '80s—New England rolls, BLT rolls, Spicy Devil rolls, Shrimp rolls, you name it. If you just wanted a tail, you could get it.

Jade from *Forbidden Fruit* leaned against the outdoor bar. I almost didn't recognize her with her clothes on. She looked every bit as good in the daylight as she did in the dim club.

She was with some tool bag, and judging by her body language, it didn't look like she wanted to be near the guy. He said something, and Jade's brow lifted with offense. I couldn't hear what she said, but it probably wasn't nice. Jade stormed off, and he grabbed her arm. She jerked free and pointed a manicured nail at him. "Don't you ever touch me!"

"Oh, my bad. I guess I didn't pay enough upfront."

I launched out of my seat. "Is there a problem here?"

"Why don't you mind your own fucking business, man?"

This guy was all of 5'8" and 130 pounds. He was barking up the wrong tree. Those little guys can get scrappy on you, but this guy wasn't one of them.

I flashed my badge. "How about you beat it?"

"It's a free country. I can have a drink."

"Touch her again, and I'll take you down."

He raised his hands innocently. "I'm just gonna sit here and mind my own business. I'm not gonna let this little tramp ruin my evening."

"I think you should apologize."

"What? Is it illegal to call a whore a whore?"

Jade's eyes narrowed. "The guy buys me a drink, and he thinks my panties are going to come off."

"They do at the club," he muttered.

She growled at him and wanted to sling her purse at him, but I pulled her away.

"Let it slide."

She took a breath and regained her composure. "You're right. He's not worth my time." She looked up at me with her sultry green eyes. "Thank you for defending my honor, Deputy."

"My pleasure."

"Would you be a doll and walk me back to my car? I don't want that creeper following me."

"Not a problem."

I gave a nod to JD and motioned that I would be back. I escorted Jade out of the restaurant, and we strolled down the boardwalk as the sun plunged below the horizon. Her high heels clacked the planks.

"Who was that guy? Did he just come up to the bar and start hassling you?"

She looked down sheepishly. "We matched on Duo and agreed to meet for a cocktail."

Duo was a popular dating app.

I lifted a surprised brow. "You matched with that guy?"

She shrugged, embarrassed. "He looked cute in his profile picture. Not so much in real life. Everybody uses filters these days."

"You need to be more careful. You never know who you're going to run into."

"I'm glad I ran into you. That guy was giving me serious creeper vibes."

We left the boardwalk and headed down Bowfin Street, then turned onto Damselfish. It was a dim avenue shrouded by a canopy of oaks that extended over the lane. There were sidewalks on either side.

"What are you doing on a dating site? I'm sure you have plenty of offers in the real world."

"I work in a strip club, Deputy. I don't date clients. And I work so much that I don't have time to meet people. The club scene is fun, but most of the guys are just idiots. It's hard to find someone of substance. Then, when you tell them what you do for a living, they either think they can demand certain things from you, or they don't want anything to do with you. And most of them grow insanely jealous."

"I'm sure you have other career opportunities."

"I'm evaluating my options. But I've got to use this money-maker while I've got it." She said with a cutesy smile and a hip shake.

She was a little heartbreaker. That was certain. She looked up at me with those inviting eyes, and the pale light glowed her porcelain skin. Her beauty was distracting.

That was about the time I noticed a guy in a Santa suit walking straight toward us on the sidewalk.

52

S anta had a sack slung over his shoulder, but it didn't contain presents. It looked like it contained a flamethrower.

He reached into his waistband and drew a 9mm.

I stepped in front of Jade, drew my pistol. "Drop the weapon! Coconut County."

Muzzle flash flickered from the barrel as he turned and ran.

It was poorly aimed harassment fire.

The bullets snapped through the air. One hit an oak tree, blasting chips of bark in all directions. The other smacked the sidewalk and sparked.

I asked Jade if she was okay.

She looked at me with startled eyes and nodded. Her body trembled. I looked her over for any injuries, then gave chase.

The scumbag sprinted down the sidewalk and took a right at the corner.

I followed with caution.

We weren't far from Oyster Avenue.

Santa sprinted down the sidewalk, angled the weapon back at me, and fired two more shots.

I ducked as the bullets ricocheted away.

He raced past a tattoo shop and took a left at the corner by a liquor store, then darted across the street. He dashed into a gravel parking lot and slipped between the rows of cars.

The gravel crunched under my feet as I followed.

Santa slid through a hole in the fence and took off down an alley toward Oyster Avenue. The little bastard was fast.

I squeezed through the fence slot, sprinted down the alley past dumpsters and trash bins, then merged onto Oyster Avenue.

That's where I had a real problem.

A crowd of spectators lined the sidewalk, watching the parade of holiday floats. There were art cars painted in Christmas themes and elves on floats, making toys. A crew of charity Santas marched down the lane.

I lost the scumbag somewhere in the crowd.

My eyes scanned the 30-odd Santas marching in unison down the street. Some of them had bags of toys, some of them didn't. They were led by a team of reindeer—*guys dressed up in reindeer suits.*

I flashed my badge, stepped into the street, and held up the parade, examining each of the Santas.

I was met by jeers from the crowd and the wanna-be Kris Kringles.

Some were portly, some were thin. Some were short, others were tall. I could be staring right at the killer and not know it. I looked for any shouldering a bag that could have contained a flamethrower.

"I need everybody to show me their waistband," I shouted.

There were groans among the jolly fellows.

"Lift up your coats now!"

They all complied, and I didn't see any 9mm pistols wedged in between red trousers and beer bellies.

Then I caught a glimpse of a Santa hat on the opposite sidewalk.

Maybe our perp had dashed through the parade of Santas and slipped into the crowd on the other side of the street.

I crossed over, snatched the hat, and kept pushing through the crowd.

The parade moved on, and I continued down the avenue, glancing down alleyways, peering into bars and restaurants.

The Slayer could have been anywhere.

I gave up the hunt after a few minutes and returned to find Jade.

She wasn't where I left her.

I didn't blame her for not sticking around. She probably got into her car and got the hell out of there.

I called the sheriff and updated him as I hustled back to Lobster Lucy's and rejoined JD.

"Every couple he's attacked, the woman has been a brunette," Jack said after I filled him in.

"Denise is right. He's following a pattern. He's selecting victims that remind him of someone. An ex-girlfriend, perhaps."

"These are all practice runs. Soon, he'll go after the ex," JD theorized. "We need to find this guy ASAP."

"Tell me something I don't know."

"You think you were targeted specifically or was this a random chance?"

"Random chance. He seemed surprised when I pulled out a gun."

We grabbed something to eat, then headed down to the station, and I filled out a report.

Daniels poked his head into the conference room. "You two need to get over to 722 Ivy Ridge Lane."

"What's going on?"

"Neighbors heard shots fired. Somebody torched the house. This could be your guy."

JD and I bolted out of the station. *Well, I bolted, JD hobbled.* We hopped into the Porsche and headed over to Ivy Ridge. I drove.

Lights flickered from emergency vehicles. Several patrol units were already on the scene. Firefighters doused the flames that crackled high into the night sky, billowing smoke across the entire island.

A crowd of curious neighbors gawked.

News crews captured the towering flames.

Tango One and media helicopters circled overhead.

It was so crowded, we had to park all the way down the street. I hopped out, and we rushed to the scene. You couldn't get too close—the heat was intense, and the fire department struggled with the blaze. The house had gone up like dried kindling.

The air was thick with a toxic soup of insulation, fabric, fire retardant, and other household chemicals. I used my shirt to cover my nose and mouth, but it didn't do much good.

I talked to Deputy Erickson. "A neighbor said he saw a guy in a Santa suit ring the doorbell. He shot the homeowner, then marched inside and capped off several more rounds."

"How many people were inside?"

"We're trying to figure that out now. Apparently, they were having a Christmas party."

Erickson frowned and shook his head. "Disgusting."

"Who's the homeowner?"

"The house belongs to Mr. and Mrs. Fletcher."

"Where's the neighbor who saw the Santa?"

He pointed to a tall gentleman in his mid 50s. Mark Wells had a narrow face, a slender build, and his hair was starting to gray on the sides. He was talking to Deputy Mendoza. We stepped to him, flashed our badges, and made introductions.

Tears streamed down Mark's face. "The Fletchers were such good people. Their daughter, Samantha, had just gotten engaged. Real nice guy, too."

I had no doubt after a rampage like this, there would be no survivors.

My mind started to turn with possibilities. "How well did you know Samantha?"

"Watched her grow up, mostly. The Fletcher's have lived here the last 20 years."

The firefighters finally got the blaze under control. The remains still smoldered and the air smelled of wet soot and ash. Arson investigators sifted through the rubble, and Brenda had the unenviable task of examining the charred remains. We all waited for the grim body count.

A young woman arrived on the scene claiming to be a close friend of Samantha's. She'd seen the blaze on the news. Her eyes were red and puffy, and tears streamed down her cheeks.

53

"Please tell me they're not all dead," the woman said in between sobs.

She was mid 20s with dark hair and olive eyes.

"We don't know yet, ma'am," I said. "What's your name?"

Her chest heaved and jerked with sobs, and she screamed with sorrow. She was on the verge of hyperventilating.

"My name is Lily."

"And what is your relationship to Samantha Fletcher?"

"She's my best friend."

It took a moment for her to get her sobbing under control, but even then, control wasn't an accurate word.

"We believe this may be related to the Santa Slayer."

"Troy," she said without hesitation.

"Who?"

"Troy Chapman. Her ex-boyfriend."

"Why do you say that?"

"Because the guy is a freak. I thought he might have had something to do with the other killings. But I dismissed it as just my imagination. I should have said something sooner. This is all my fault." She broke down into sobs again.

"It's not your fault. Tell me about Troy."

"He didn't handle the breakup well. Then when he found out about the engagement, I think he went over the edge. Samantha said he's been calling and harassing her lately. Making veiled threats."

"You know where we can find Troy?"

"He used to live in the Summer Sands apartments. I don't know if he still does. He's so weird. Every year for Halloween, he would dress up as an Evil Santa. That's why I thought of him when that first couple was torched at Fort Dawson."

Faulkner interrupted. "The neighbor next to Mark Wells has a video doorbell. I managed to export footage."

He showed me the clip on his phone. It caught an angle of a man in a Santa suit, missing a cap, walking down the street with a flamethrower. He marched to the Fletchers' door and rang the bell. When Mr. Fletcher opened, muzzle flash flickered. Fletcher fell to the floor, and Santa marched inside and delivered his wicked presents.

I reviewed the footage a few times. I couldn't be certain from the angle. I couldn't see the man's face behind the fake beard and the sunglasses, but I was pretty sure it was the same sick Santa that had attacked Jade and me earlier.

I showed the footage to Lily. "That's Troy. No doubt."

I said to JD, "Let's see if we can get a warrant for this scumbag."

"With any luck, Brenda will find his body among the remains," JD muttered.

"I don't see this guy taking his own life. He's too enamored with himself."

We headed back to the station, and Lily gave a sworn affidavit that the man in the video was Troy Chapman.

After reviewing the footage, Judge Echols disagreed. He said from the angle, it was impossible to determine the identity of the killer.

I contained my anger and tried to focus.

Just because we didn't have a warrant didn't mean we couldn't knock on the dirtbag's door and ask him a few questions.

54

We pulled Troy Chapman's records and paid him a visit at the Summer Sands apartments. It was a mid-rise complex with parking underneath and a small visitors' lot. It was a couple of blocks off the beach. If you lived on the good side of the building and paid a premium, you had a decent view.

He lived on the third floor on the good side. The units weren't cheap. Well, nothing on the island was cheap. Even the roach traps were overpriced.

I put a heavy fist against the door. "Coconut County! Open up."

I found that if you speak with authority, most people will often comply.

I banged on the door again and waited.

Still, there was no response.

The elevator doors slid open a moment later, and the rumble drew my eye down the long hallway. Lo-and-behold,

Troy Chapman rounded the corner wearing a ratty Santa suit carrying a sack that contained nothing but a flamethrower. It was obvious from the outline.

His eyes rounded. He spun around and darted back the way he came. I heard him push into the stairwell, and his boots smacked the concrete.

I gave chase. JD didn't really run, and he didn't really walk. He just shuffled.

My legs drove me forward as I sprinted down the hall and rounded the corner by the elevators. I pushed through the steel fire door and darted down the switchback staircase.

The deafening blast from a 9mm echoed as Troy popped off a round.

I ducked as the bullet smacked the cinderblock wall, sending chips and debris scattering. In the confined space, the bang was extra loud and rang my ears.

He continued his descent, and I followed cautiously.

When he hit the bottom landing, he pushed through a door that exited into the parking lot under the building.

I followed moments after.

A woman had pulled into the parking garage with her child. She was driving a small black four-door sedan.

Troy had his weapon aimed at her and demanded access to the vehicle. As soon as he saw me exit the stairwell, he swung the barrel in my direction and popped off two rounds.

The bullet snapped through the air, and I ducked for cover behind a parked car. A bullet shattered a window, sprinkling shards of glass. The other hit a body panel, leaving a nice round hole in the door.

Troy hopped into the backseat of the black four-door sedan and forced the woman at gunpoint to drive away. She raced past me with terrified eyes. She turned for the exit, waiting momentarily for the gate to open.

I made note of the license plate and called Sheriff Daniels.

By that time, JD had joined me in the garage. We rushed around to the visitor lot and hopped into the Porsche.

I drove.

The under building parking exited on Piping Rock. I saw the vehicle speed away as I cranked up the engine. I pulled out of the parking space and gave chase.

"Do not wreck my car," JD cautioned as he grabbed the door handle.

I smashed the accelerator to the floor, and the engine howled. The turbos whined, and we pulled within a few car lengths of the black sedan in no time.

I called Troy Chapman's cell phone, but he'd been smart enough to keep it off during the killings. I wasn't sure if he even carried it on him. It rang a few times, then went to voicemail.

I called Denise and had her run the plates to the sedan. The car belonged to Kelly Bennett. Denise looked up her cell number, and I gave her a call. It rang a few times with no answer.

I immediately dialed again, and still no answer.

I handed my phone to JD, and he sent a text identifying ourselves as police officers and that Troy should talk to us if he wanted to negotiate a safe resolution for all.

I followed the sedan as it twisted through the streets of Coconut Key—not driving particularly fast, but not slow either.

JD handed the phone back to me, and I tried calling Kelly's number again.

Troy finally picked up the phone. "What do you want?"

"Troy, this is going to end badly for you."

"Back off, or these good people die."

"How do you plan on getting out of this scenario? You're only making it worse for yourself."

"Leave me alone, or these hostages die."

I heard shrieks and cries in the background.

"You don't want to hurt those people. They've done nothing to you."

"As you can see from my history, I don't have a problem hurting innocent people."

"I noticed. You killed your ex-girlfriend's entire family."

"They deserved it."

"I think that's an argument you're going to have a hard time winning."

Tango One thumped overhead, and its spotlight slashed the night air, illuminating the black sedan with a bluish beam of blinding light.

"What part of back off do you not understand?" Troy barked.

Several patrol cars fell in line behind us with flashing red and blues, sirens wailing.

"Is English your second language? I want the helicopter and the patrol cars gone. If they don't disappear within the next 60 seconds, I'm putting a bullet into this adorable little girl."

She shrieked and cried.

"That won't be necessary," I said. "I can get them to back off, but they're going to need to see a show of good faith. How about you let the little girl go, and I'll make the helicopter and the patrol units disappear?"

"You're out of your mind if you think I'm going to stop this vehicle and let someone out."

"Sounds like you're concerned."

"You're damn right! I'm concerned if I allow this car to stop, your deputies will swarm in."

"I can give you my word that they won't. I'll play fair with you if you play fair with me.

"We're going to run out of gas soon," the woman said, her voice barely filtering through the speaker.

"I'm disappointed, Troy. I thought we had a rapport. But you tried to kill me earlier on Damselfish."

"That was you?"

"Yep."

"Sorry about that. Random target."

"I don't think your targets are all that random." I paused. "Look, I'm trying to help you. If you don't want my help, fine. But you're quickly running out of options."

He was silent for a long moment. "Here's the deal. I'll let the girl out at the next stoplight. You guys back off, and nobody hassles me while we fill it up with gas. You got me?"

"I got you. I'll tell my people."

I ended the call, then dialed Sheriff Daniels. I relayed the terms, and he agreed.

Tango One peeled away.

The red and blues stopped flashing, and the deputies hung back out of view.

I kept following the black sedan, as agreed. At the next red light, the door opened, and a terrified 10-year-old sprinted to the sidewalk. The light turned green, and the black sedan sped away.

The girl on the corner sobbed and cried.

We pulled alongside her, and JD flashed his badge.

She shook her head and ran away, not believing he was a cop.

She ran down a side street, and I had a deputy in a patrol car chase after her. He finally recovered the girl and convinced her to get into the squad car with him.

I lost sight of the black sedan during that time, but a call to Isabella saved the day. She was able to track Kelly's cell phone in real-time.

They had pulled into a gas station a few blocks away and were sitting at the pump when we pulled onto the scene.

Troy pulled the woman out of the car and forced her to use her credit card, adding insult to injury. She pumped gas while Troy kept the pistol on her.

At the next pump over, a guy was filling up his diesel truck when the whole thing went down. His eyes narrowed at the Evil Santa.

Troy's nervous eyes flicked about. He shouted to the patrons. "Nobody move, or she dies!"

Kelly kept pumping the gas.

"Come on, let's go!" Troy shouted at her.

The tank was almost full.

Troy kept an eye on the guy with the diesel truck. Mr. Diesel didn't seem pleased about the situation and looked like the type that might do something about it.

Mr. Diesel was enough of a distraction for Troy that Kelly saw an opportunity. She removed the nozzle and sprayed Troy in the face with gasoline.

Most modern nozzles have an attitude sensor, which is just a ball bearing that shuts off the pump. But they don't always work, and this was an older station.

Troy clutched his stinging eyes while Kelly took off running.

Like a dumbass, Troy took aim and fired his weapon at her. With eyes full of petrol, his aim was shit.

But that was the least of his worries.

The spark ignited the gasoline, and Troy lit up. Amber flames engulfed his body. He flailed about, screeching and wailing. His skin sizzled and crackled, and the putrid stench of burning flesh mixed with the smell of fuel.

Patrons scattered, anticipating the worst.

The attendant hit the emergency shutoff, then dashed out with a fire extinguisher. He doused the flaming Santa with CO_2.

Sirens warbled in the distance.

By some miracle, the station didn't go up in flames.

EMTs and firefighters were on the scene in minutes. But by that time, Troy Chapman was a lump of coal. And I can't say too many were upset about that.

First responders swarmed the scene, and Troy's remains still smoldered. The news crews arrived, and helicopters circled overhead.

Kelly was reunited with her daughter.

Paris Delaney found me. She didn't drag her crew with her. They were busy grabbing footage of the charred corpse. "I guess I owe you $100. You solved the Lights in the Heights case, you exposed a corrupt military contractor, and you got the Slayer."

"I guess my reputation is still intact."

"It appears so," she said with a smile before sauntering away.

After we wrapped up, JD and I headed to the station, filled out reports, then called it a night.

It had been a long few days, and I was more than ready for a holiday break. I figured we deserved a little time off. But somebody is always causing trouble in Coconut Key.

Paris continued to cover the *Lights in the Heights* story. Neither Carol nor Esther won. The grand prize went to Norah Bailey. Esther came in third behind Carol. Paris interviewed Norah, and she was understandably over the moon with her recent accomplishment.

"It's not about winning or losing," Esther said on camera as Paris interviewed her. "It's about the season and giving. I'm happy for Norah. She deserves the win." Then she added, "There's always next year."

Carol interrupted the interview and apologized for everything. The two women embraced and shed a few tears. I think they were well on their way to burying the hatchet.

Scarlett got out of rehab, and we celebrated the season on the boat with a feast fit for kings. The usual suspects gathered—Sheriff Daniels, Teagan, Denise, Scarlett, and the guys in the band. JD had the meal catered in and hired hotties in skimpy elf costumes to serve the food and beverages. A quartet played Christmas classics, and eggnog flowed.

There were so many presents under the tree, you could barely move in the salon. After we ate and drank our fill, we passed out packages and tore into the wrapping paper. The place was a mess in no time, but the delighted faces were priceless.

JD bought the band all new equipment—guitars, basses, amps, speaker cabinets, drums, cymbals, and a new PA system.

The guys in the band were beside themselves.

The theft of their gear had left everyone pretty bummed. But this definitely brightened their spirits. Now they had everything needed to pull off their New Year's Eve show without a hitch.

We were determined to nab the gear thieves. Their day would come.

We soaked up a few leisurely days after Christmas. We lounged, drank, chased skirts, and searched for the lost treasure that we had found and lost again. We had no luck with the treasure but did okay with the skirts.

Jenson was looking at accessory to murder, a co-conspirator in the kidnapping of a law enforcement officer, and a host of other felonies.

DCIS investigators were able to recover data from the West-Tek hard drives. After scrutinizing emails and text messages, along with Preston's statement, they determined Alexandria had no knowledge of the coverup. The contract for the AIBCIS was canceled. West-Tek was in ruin.

Though the federal investigation was ongoing, no further indictments were made. I suspected a few co-conspirators would walk away unscathed. *Somebody started that fire.* But Preston and Jenson wouldn't see daylight anytime soon.

Autumn Clark was never apprehended. I'm not sure if she fled the country or was *disappeared*.

I talked to Alexandria once after everything went down. She maintained her innocence and denied everything. Did she have any involvement? Who really knows. I figured she'd rise from the ashes of West-Tek and start a new company. She was an ambitious woman and knew how to grease the right palms.

Wild Fury rocked the strip on New Year's Eve, and the after-party raged beyond sunrise. It took a few days to recover. By that time, JD wasn't hobbling anymore. He'd nursed his wounds and was getting back into fighting shape. It was a good thing, too. Only a couple days into the new year, someone else was dead. And we had a most unusual case to solve.

Ready for more?

The adventure continues with Wild Target!

Join my newsletter and find out what happens next!

AUTHOR'S NOTE

Thanks for all the great reviews!

I've got more adventures for Tyson and JD. Stay tuned.

If you liked this book, let me know with a review on Amazon.

Thanks for reading!

—*Tripp*

TYSON WILD

Wild Ocean

Wild Justice

Wild Rivera

Wild Tide

Wild Rain

Wild Captive

Wild Killer

Wild Honor

Wild Gold

Wild Case

Wild Crown

Wild Break

Wild Fury

Wild Surge

Wild Impact

Wild L.A.

Wild High

Wild Abyss

Wild Life

Wild Spirit

Wild Thunder

Wild Season

Wild Rage

Wild Heart

Wild Spring

Wild Outlaw

Wild Revenge

Wild Secret

Wild Envy

Wild Surf

Wild Venom

Wild Island

Wild Demon

Wild Blue

Wild Lights

Wild Target

Wild...

CONNECT WITH ME

I'm just a geek who loves to write. Follow me on Facebook.

www.trippellis.com

Made in the USA
Middletown, DE
30 November 2021

53810417R00187